Meet the team:

Alex – A quiet lad from Nor.... team in survival skills. His dad is in the SAS and Alex is determined to follow in his footsteps, whatever it takes. He who dares . . .

Li – Expert in martial arts and free-climbing, Li can get to grips with most situations . . .

Paulo – The laid-back Argentinian is a mechanical genius, and with his medical skills he can patch up injuries as well as motors . . .

Hex – An ace hacker, Hex is first rate at code-breaking and can bypass most security systems . . .

Amber – Her top navigational skills mean the team are rarely lost. Rarely lost for words either, rich-girl Amber can show some serious attitude . . .

With plenty of hard work and training, together they are Alpha Force – an elite squad of young people dedicated to combating injustice throughout the world.

In *Fault Line* Alpha Force are in Belize and an earthquake is about to hit . . .

www.kidsatrandomhouse.co.uk/alphaforce

chris
ALPHA FORCE
Ryan

FAULT LINE

ALPHA FORCE: FAULT LINE
A RED FOX BOOK 0 099 48015 8

First published in Great Britain by Red Fox,
an imprint of Random House Children's Books

This edition published 2005

1 3 5 7 9 10 8 6 4 2

Papers used by Random House Children's Books are natural, recyclable
products made from wood grown in sustainable forests. The manufacturing
processes conform to the environmental regulations of the country of origin.

Typeset in Sabon by Palimpsest Book Production Limited,
Polmont, Stirlingshire

Red Fox Books are published by Random House Children's Books,
61–63 Uxbridge Road, London W5 5SA,
a division of The Random House Group Ltd,
in Australia by Random House Australia (Pty) Ltd,
20 Alfred Street, Milsons Point, Sydney, NSW 2061, Australia,
in New Zealand by Random House New Zealand Ltd,
18 Poland Road, Glenfield, Auckland 10, New Zealand,
and in South Africa by Random House (Pty) Ltd,
Endulini, 5A Jubilee Road, Parktown 2193, South Africa

THE RANDOM HOUSE GROUP Limited Reg. No. 954009
www.kidsatrandomhouse.co.uk

A CIP catalogue record for this book is available from the British Library.

Printed and bound in Great Britain by
Cox & Wyman Ltd, Reading, Berkshire

ALPHA FORCE

The field of
operation...

NORTH
AMERICA

BELIZE

AFRICA

SOUTH
AMERICA

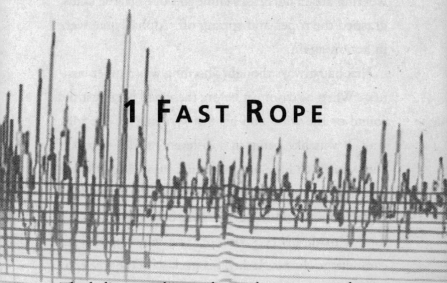

1 FAST ROPE

The helicopter skimmed over the grey-green forest. Its downdraught left a wake through the treetops like a ship's through an ocean. Jungle birds took off in flashes of blue, red and white. Occasionally a river could be seen far below, a pale silver thread; otherwise there was nothing below the 10.5-tonne Puma helicopter but endless dark jungle-green.

Belize, central America.

The heli pulled around in a wide circle, slowed and hovered. Five ropes dropped from the open cabin and unfurled down to the tree canopy. Five figures wearing abseil harnesses climbed out onto the skids, grasped the ropes and sprang off. Alpha Force were in action again.

Hex had always thought abseiling was a quiet business. When he'd done it before there had been just the sound of the wind and his feet scraping on the rock wall. It was like being in a different world – great if you wanted to have a good think. Hex liked solitary activities, but now his ears were full of the high whine of the engine and the drumming of rotor blades, so loud it made his eyes vibrate. The wind rippled his camouflage clothes, lashed his neck with the free ends of the straps on his green bergen backpack. There was nothing for his feet to walk on – just thin air. He had one hand on the rope above, one hand on the free end below, following the line into the deep green trees.

He looked at his friends, sliding down from the Puma like spiders down a thread. Amber's bright pink abseil harness looked like a Barbie accessory next to her disruption-patterned jungle camouflage – not the kind of thing you could tell her and still be alive afterwards. Hex grinned. OK, maybe you could have useful thoughts while your ears were being drilled.

Li's slight frame was dwarfed by her bergen. She slipped down the rope with the grace of a trapeze artist, as though it was perfectly natural to be in mid air. She was grinning at Paulo, challenging him to see who would get down faster. Li was never happier than when racing someone. Paulo, the big Argentinian, normally the most laid-back of the group, was giving her a run for her money. His natural habitat was on horseback, cantering lazily across the plains on his family's ranch but Li never failed to get him going.

Opposite him, Alex checked the winch man in the heli above, then looked down at the green tree canopy approaching below. He did his job quietly and expertly, planning what they needed to do when they hit bottom.

Hex's eye slid back to Amber in her Barbie harness, her sleeves rolled up and her ebony arms working the ropes briskly, as though she would take no nonsense from them.

His feet touched the topmost leaves of the trees. Time to concentrate.

* * *

During the freefall, moments before they hit the trees, Amber smiled. What could you tell about someone from the colour of harness they chose? Alex had a green one – unobtrusive, blending in. Anglo-Chinese Li wore red – the Chinese colour of luck, and fiery too. Appropriate in two ways. The other two had chosen black. Paulo, macho Latin-American, good looking – of course he'd go for black. But what about Hex? The hacker from inner-city London. He was probably more at home in the Matrix than surrounded by trees and sky. Black for a loner from planet cyberspace.

She looked at Li and Paulo. They were already shoulder-deep in the tree canopy, proceeding slowly. They were still fifteen metres above the ground and had to follow the rope where it threaded between the branches – the trickiest part of the descent. Alex was waist-deep, going down in careful stages.

Amber felt large leaves touch her feet, brush her shins. She slowed.

Slipping into the canopy was like going under water. The baking sun disappeared; wet leaves left cool trails on her skin. Even the beat of the rotor

4

blades became muffled. The foliage swished as she descended. Next to her was a solid tree trunk more than a metre wide.

She dodged away from a protruding branch and glanced up. There were the five lines quivering like guitar strings. High above in the heli, the winch man was watching to see when they reached the ground, his yellow-gloved hands steadying the drum that held the ropes. All was well.

She saw a flash of red through the foliage below her, four metres to her right; that must be Li. She must be nearly down, but the jungle was already so dense she couldn't see any more than the harness. The camouflage clothes were doing their job. The whereabouts of the others was betrayed only by the quivering leaves and the sound of breaking branches. Even Hex, who had been barely a metre and a half away from her when standing on the skid, was hidden by a tree trunk.

'Come on,' called a voice. Li. 'Are you guys staying up there all day?' Her rope rose through the trees, a red snake rustling vertically up as the winch man reeled it back in, becoming a black thread against the sky. She must have touched down.

'I seem to have got the most complicated tree in the jungle.' A Geordie accent. That was Alex. 'I thought this was meant to be a quick way of getting down.'

'It is,' called Li. 'If you get lucky with your route.'

Amber felt a gentle tug on her harness. The heli drifted above like a tethered balloon.

Then she saw something that made her heart turn a somersault.

The helicopter tilted. The winch man was thrown forwards. For a moment his arms and legs were out of the door, then his harness caught him and he scrambled back in. Was the heli in trouble?

Paulo felt something jerk him upwards violently. It stopped again just as suddenly. He grabbed a branch and clung on, then looked up.

The heli was wobbling in the air. The winch man was holding onto the doorway, his arms and legs braced. The pilot seemed to be fighting to keep control.

Paulo went cold all over. Was it about to come down? If it did, they didn't stand a chance. He yelled to the others, 'The heli's in trouble. Go go go!'

He let the rope slip him further down, not being so careful now. He had about ten metres to go and he had to get down fast.

He descended a few centimetres and was jerked up again, hard. His head cracked against a branch. The blow made his head buzz. Go down, said his brain. He tried again.

Yet again he was yanked up. What was going on? He had to get away. He tried again.

He was dragged back up the rough tree like a sack on a crane.

Dios, why couldn't he get away? It was like a bad dream.

Above him, the heli rocked in the sky. It looked like an ornament about to topple off a shelf.

Now his abseil rope was stuck. He couldn't move down at all. He was helplessly attached to the great big machine. He imagined rotor blades chopping towards him like a giant windmill, spilling fuel that would ignite the trees in an orange fireball.

He saw ropes snaking up into the belly of the craft. The others had reached the ground. He was the only one still attached to the heli now, and like some tentacled monster in its death throes it wouldn't let him go.

The winch man was waving frantically, yellow gloves trying to get his attention. Paulo suddenly realized that the problem was him. His line must be tangled. The rope below him must have got wrapped around a branch. Whenever the heli drifted on an air current, it was yanked back by a big, solid tree. Paulo was on a tug-of-war rope between the two. And his earlier instinct had been right: if he didn't act quickly, the heli would definitely come down.

Paulo looked down. Below was dense foliage. He couldn't even see the rope, let alone where it was tangled. He'd have to tell the winch man to cut him free.

He worked like lightning. He had a spare lanyard on his harness; a short length of rope with a kara-biner clip. He grabbed a branch, hooked it around and tested it. Yes, it would take his weight. He clipped his harness onto it, looked up at the winch man and drew his hand across his neck in a throat-slitting motion.

The winch man was ready for his signal. He cut

the rope immediately and it came snaking down towards Paulo. Paulo grabbed for it and the heli lifted away, moving smoothly and safely once more. Then he tied the free end of the rope around the branch in a figure-of-eight knot. His heart was hammering so hard his hands shook and it took a few goes to loop the rope back into the karabiner. He'd nearly brought the helicopter down.

Now he had secured the rope, he could continue abseiling – once he'd untangled the end. He pulled it up and glimpsed a big purple knot. This was going to take some time. Perhaps it was just what he needed to help him calm down – something monotonous, like knitting in reverse. He sighed and got to work.

2 THE MISSION

When Paulo finally reached the bottom of the tree his four friends were sitting on their bergens drinking from their water bottles.

'I thought you'd decided to stay up there,' said Li.

Alex looked at his watch. 'Twenty minutes. I reckon that must be the world record for the slowest fast-rope.'

Li screwed the top back on her water bottle. 'I think next time I race you, I'll have a snooze first and then catch you up.'

Paulo was drenched in sweat. He shrugged his

bergen off his back and took off his harness. But he wasn't so far gone that he couldn't give as good as he got from Li. 'The whole point,' he said to her, 'was to be the last down, not the first.' He peeled off his abseiling gloves; they had moulded themselves to him like a second skin.

'You should have seen Hex,' grinned Amber. 'One moment, I didn't know where any of you were. The next, he was shinning down a tree like a rat down a drainpipe.'

'Closely followed by you,' Hex rejoined. Her pink harness was lying on the ground next to her bergen. Hex picked it up and put his hands through the leg holes, flapping his hands to mime someone running very fast on tiptoe.

Amber snatched the harness from him and swiped him with it before stuffing it into the top of her bergen.

Paulo drank some water, leaned back against a tree and breathed a long sigh of relief.

Then he froze.

A snake hung down from a tree. It had a dark brown body the colour of tree bark, but the underside was bright yellow. The yellow edged its mouth like a thick coat of lipstick. It hissed at him, the inside of its mouth glossy black, like patent leather. 'That's all I need,' he said softly.

'Wow,' breathed Li. 'A vine snake.'

Paulo remained stock-still, his neck twisted round, staring at the snake. 'Yes, but is it—?'

'It's not poisonous,' said Li.

Paulo believed her; her parents were naturalists and she knew her flora and fauna. But all the same, he stayed exactly where he was.

'There,' said Li. 'It's going already.'

The snake slithered down the tree and disappeared into the undergrowth. Paulo relaxed.

Amber pulled the map out of her belt kit and unfolded it on the forest floor. 'Well, guys – we're on our own. Seven days until we see the heli again.'

'We'll try not to pull it out of the sky when we see it,' said Li, and dragged Paulo towards the map.

They hunkered down to get their bearings. The map showed just dense jungle – no paths, no signs of civilization. Probably no human had set foot there for centuries. This place belonged to the birds, small mammals, snakes and insects. Now the five friends would be living by their wits and their skills.

It felt like the holidays had really started. The rest of the time they were all at various schools all over the globe – Alex in Northumberland; Li in whatever corner of the globe her parents were working in; Paulo in Argentina; Hex in London; and Amber in the US. But now they were together and they were Alpha Force again.

Ever since they'd been thrown together on a ship sailing around Indonesia, this was what holidays were about. The five teenagers had been marooned on a tropical island and disaster had followed disaster. They had to live off the land, fighting hostile wildlife. When a rescue boat arrived it turned out to be crewed by a vicious band of pirates – and their struggle to survive became all-out war. When they finally came through, none of them would ever be the same again.

But there was more to that summer than survival. When they'd fought off the pirates, they had saved the lives of a French family. It was a turning point for all of them. Together, they could help people.

Their muddled teenage lives suddenly had purpose; Amber in particular felt able to face the world for the first time since her parents had died on an undercover mission. The five knew they had found their raison d'être. Alpha Force was formed in memory of Amber's mother and father – and to carry on their work helping disadvantaged people.

Every school holiday Alpha Force came together to face different challenges. They were helped by Amber's uncle, her guardian John Middleton. He'd arranged the helicopter they'd come in on, persuading a friend in an oil company to let them hitch a ride on one of the craft used to ferry workers to the offshore rigs. John Middleton had been a key player in her parents' missions – using his powerful friends to organize and fund missions and provide equipment. He was pleased when his niece had found an interest in life through her new friends. He was happy to pull a few strings if it kept her amused and would even rustle up demanding challenges for them, such as breaking into a secure military building. He would not have been so willing if he'd known that Alpha Force's 'challenges' were often as deadly as the missions of Amber's parents.

Right now, their challenge was a seven-day trek through the deepest jungle – to refresh survival skills and hone their navigation techniques.

The map was unlike any they'd seen before. On most maps there were tracks, railway lines and rock features; here there was nothing. Just a big area marked with wavy red contour lines, height markers and the odd tree symbol. Endless, featureless jungle.

Li sat up and slapped her palms against her thighs decisively. 'That's enough of being lost. Hex, just get out your box of tricks and tell us where we are.'

Hex carried a sophisticated palmtop computer on his belt. It could do many amazing things – one of which was to use satellites to calculate precisely where they were – a global positioning system. But he wasn't using it. 'No good,' he said. 'The tree canopy here's too thick. It can't punch through.'

'Damn,' said Li. 'Thought I could tempt you to try.'

'For this trip it's old-fashioned map and compass, I'm afraid,' said Alex. He identified where they were from a grid reference taken in the heli and scored the map with his fingernail to mark it. 'You can't always rely on boxes of tricks. There are times when GPS might not work.' But he knew they all understood the importance of this exercise. In the kinds of places they worked in, they might find themselves stranded without any equipment. And as they would probably be coping with all sorts of other problems – such as surviving – their navigation skills had to be second nature.

Alex stood up. 'Ready to go?'

They shouldered their bergens and got into single file. Completing this exercise would take teamwork. There were clear roles: Paulo would go first; Amber and Alex would follow with a map each, checking and double-checking the route – with no horizon to help them and no landmarks, sticking to the map was vital; Li and Hex would bring up the rear, keeping track of how far they had travelled.

'Follow the ridge,' said Amber to Paulo.

Paulo looked down at his feet. There was a ridge, easy to see because it was used as a track by animals; but it forked into a Y shape. 'Which one?'

Amber and Alex consulted their maps. They

hadn't even set off but the tiniest detail, easy to miss, could make all the difference. 'Left,' said Alex.

Paulo walked on. After a little while, the ground to the left fell away into a steep slope.

Alex looked at the map. 'Is that marked?'

Amber looked at her map. Everything had to be checked. She nodded, showing it to Alex. 'Yes. This ridge line. Looks like it's nearly a hundred metres deep.'

'*Dios*,' said Paulo. He suddenly had visions of blundering over a precipice, his heavy bergen pulling him over like a lead weight. He'd thought the jungle would all be flat. He'd have to be careful where he put his feet.

Hex seemed to read his thoughts. 'Just when you think it's getting boring.'

'You know what?' said Alex. 'I think there was an earthquake here. Dad said you came across places like this.'

'You're loving this, aren't you?' said Amber. 'Look at your face.'

Alex was grinning. His dad was in the SAS and had told many stories of his jungle training in Belize.

Now here Alex was, following in his footsteps. He felt very good indeed. 'Yeah,' he said. 'I like it here.'

Hex wasn't feeling quite as much at home. 'Did your dad say how often earthquakes happen here? It might be good to know.'

'I think we're OK.' Li pointed down into the valley. 'That one occurred quite a long time ago. The vegetation is well established. Those trees are at least fifty years old.'

'Quite a long time ago – or quite recent, depending on how you look at it,' said Hex.

They plodded on.

'Ten-metre check,' called Li and Hex simultaneously. This was the other vital element in the equation. As well as knowing what direction they were going in, the party also had to know how far they had travelled. On other training exercises they had learned to count their paces and judge when they'd done ten metres, adjusting for uphill or downhill slopes. Li and Hex carried hand-held clicker devices and pressed them every time they'd done ten metres, comparing the score to check they were both still accurate.

The team's roles were carefully allocated according

to their skills and aptitudes. Paulo, leading the way, had to notice whether they were going downhill or uphill. If they found themselves climbing or descending, it could mean they were going wrong. Without a horizon it was surprisingly difficult to tell, but Paulo was extra sensitive to changes in his balance after spending a lifetime in the saddle.

'Going down,' he called as he felt his feet moving faster and the bergen pushing him like a hand in his back.

Amber and Alex looked at the maps again, tracing the ridge lines. Yes, their ridge went down and the one next to it stayed level. 'Down is good,' said Amber.

Alex was a good choice for map reader because he had spent years camping alone in the Northumbrian moors where he grew up. He could look at a map and visualize the contours in three dimensions. He could tell if what looked like the shortest route would take him up a steep hill, or if he would be better taking a longer way round. The map of the Belize jungle would test this to the limit.

Amber, as second map reader, was also used to

finding her way in featureless spaces. Out on the open sea in her parents' yacht, she'd had to know exactly where she was on sea charts. Now her finely honed sense of direction was coming into its own.

Hex and Li, at the back, were the most accurate at judging distance. Li was good at it because she had trained as an athlete from an early age. She knew exactly how long her stride was and could keep it accurate. Hex was a talented hacker; his brain handled details well and he was able to lock out other thoughts and concentrate, the way he did when he was programming and one missing comma might mean disaster. He gave the job his absolute attention.

However, not all of them found their roles easy. While Alex glowed with pride, and Paulo tromped ahead in his usual happy-go-lucky way, Amber found herself longing for a breeze. The air was still and muggy. Sweat drenched her. She could have sworn moisture was pouring off the leaves onto her, otherwise why was there so much? There was no sky. When she looked up it was just deep green, with branches springing back as animals ran away from them.

Li found their progress slow and frustrating. She liked doing things fast, with the wind in her long hair and the whip of adrenaline through her veins. Her mind wanted to wander. All around her was fantastic wildlife. The jungle was literally shrieking with it: birds and animals called to each other; leaves rustled as creatures skittered away from them. She dug her toe into a mound to see if it was safe to step on and insects ran all over her black jungle boot. Even the dirt was teeming with life. With a wrench she brought her mind back to the task in hand.

But if Li longed for time to gaze around at the natural world, Hex wanted the opposite. He wasn't keen on jungles. Leaves touched his shoulders, whipped his face. Branches prodded him like nagging fingers. Vines tangled around his legs. Things hopped and scuttled out of his way. He was claustrophobic and began to feel that the trees were closing in. It was sweltering, too. It was just as well he had the pace-counting to do; otherwise he'd have been thinking about the fact that his palmtop couldn't get a signal. Their only contact with the outside world was the signal balloon they'd brought in case they needed to call for help. Hardly the state-of-the-art communications Hex was used to. Without access to the web, Hex felt very isolated indeed.

Click. Li counted another ten metres. 'Check,' she called, and Hex echoed her.

Amber cursed. Her foot was caught in something. She felt something like claws in her leg. She looked down to see a tangled mass of spiky thorns, like brambles.

'Amber, stop!' Alex said. 'Don't try and struggle. It's a wait-a-while. If you struggle you'll just get more stuck. It's like barbed wire.'

Amber stood up straight, hands on hips. 'Well what do I do? Wait for them to dissolve?'

'I'll help you.' Alex handed the map to Paulo and knelt beside Amber. He grasped one of the barbs and pushed her leg carefully back.

'Ow,' said Amber. 'That hurts.'

'Sorry. You have to unhook it back the way you came.' The first barb came out. He got to work on the second. 'This stuff used to be the bane of my dad's life.'

'You know,' said Paulo, 'I think he's pleased we've

found some because he can show us what to do. Look at his face.'

Alex tried to hide his smile but it broke out at the corners of his mouth anyway. He tried burying his chin in his collar instead.

Amber tutted with frustration. 'Well, the least you could do is thank me for enabling you to demonstrate another vital SAS survival skill,' she said. 'This stuff isn't poisonous, is it?'

Li shook her head. 'No.'

'Ow!' said Amber again, more insistently.

'Oh, quit complaining,' said Hex. 'You probably feel worse when you inject yourself.' Amber was a diabetic and had to inject herself with insulin twice a day. She carried an insulin injection kit in a small leather pouch on her belt pack.

'It's different if you do it to yourself,' she said.

'Last one,' said Alex. 'You got off lightly. Dad said you can get really stuck in these. We'd better look at the scratches when we get to camp.'

They got back in formation and walked on.

In the jungle, they knew that you could become disorientated if you didn't have complete confidence in your map and your navigators. It was easy to lose track of time. It was monotonous terrain – the same kinds of trees, the same kinds of animal noises, hour after hour. Even though Paulo was alert, when he saw the landscape change, he felt like he had been shocked out of a sleepwalk.

'What's that? Over to the left? There aren't any trees.'

The others followed where he was pointing. The trees on the right-hand side were not nearly as thick. Beyond, there seemed to be some large open space.

'Brilliant,' said Hex. 'No more trees.'

Paulo hacked into a tree with his machete, carving a shape like an arrow so they knew where to come back to. They picked their way through the vegetation. Ahead, the tree canopy disappeared and brilliant blue sky showed through. The sun shone down. It was like moving close to a fire.

Paulo was through first. 'Wow,' he said. 'Careful, I'm quite close to the edge here.'

They stepped forwards until they were level with Paulo. He was standing on the edge of a crater fifty metres wide. It was as if the floor of the jungle had fallen away and left a great circular hole, lined with limestone cliffs. Forty metres down, a still pool of water reflected the blue sky and their five faces at one edge – tiny and insignificant.

'A sinkhole,' said Alex. 'Dad told me about these. They used to abseil into them and go swimming. He said he never touched the bottom of one.'

'Typical,' snorted Amber. 'Hundreds of years ago these sinkholes were sacred to the ancient Maya civilization. They made sacrifices to the gods in them. And you guys went swimming in them.'

'Didn't know you were such a hippy,' said Hex.

Li looked at the water and imagined diving in, slipping beneath its cool surface. She grabbed Paulo's arm and made to throw him in. 'Go on, jump – I'll rescue you.'

For a moment Paulo thought she would. He imagined plummeting straight to the bottom with his bergen and ran backwards smartly. She looked at him, a teasing glint in her eye. He grinned back but he knew that if she'd really wanted to throw him in he wouldn't have got away.

The five friends looked at the water longingly.

They were so hot and sticky and it looked so refreshing.

Hex checked his watch. 'I don't want to be a spoil-sport, guys, but we haven't got our camp sorted yet and we should do that in the next hour. We don't want to be tramping through the jungle in the dark.'

Alex nodded. 'You're right. We're bound to see another sinkhole.' He led the way back to Paulo's mark.

'Anyway,' said Amber, 'we'd have to find some rope.'

'Maybe,' suggested Li, 'we'll find some abandoned in a tree – what do you think, Paulo?'

'Not a chance,' said Paulo. 'Nobody would do a thing like that.'

As they walked reluctantly away from the sinkhole, they didn't see what happened next. One moment the water was absolutely still, like a painting. Then it trembled. The entire surface shivered, as though the rocks around it had been shaken, hard. Gradually, it settled.

An earth tremor.

3 JUNGLE NIGHT

'Have you seen this?' said Hex. 'I thought you said the jungle was uninhabited.'

They had stopped in a clearing to see if it was suitable for their camp. While Li looked for water and Alex and Amber checked the tree canopy for broken branches that might fall on them, Paulo and Hex checked the ground to make sure there were no swampy patches.

Now Hex was looking at a row of stones like cobbles about a metre high. They continued in a straight line into the undergrowth.

Paulo joined him. He brushed away some earth on the top of the wall with his hands. 'It's not a wall, it's a platform.'

Hex straightened up. 'Well, the furry tree creatures didn't make that.' He put on a spooky voice. 'We are not alone.'

'I know what it is,' said Paulo. 'It's an ancient Maya settlement.' His eyes were glittering with excitement. 'This might have been a city.'

'That explains this,' said Li. She had found a hole in the limestone like a miniature well, about twenty-five centimetres in diameter and filled with water. 'Looks like it's been here a long time.' She dipped her finger in and smelled it. The water was reasonably clean. 'Not bad. We should be able to purify it.'

Alex smiled. 'We've got water, the canopy looks safe, the ground is dry . . . ideal place for a camp.'

Amber was looking at Hex's low wall. 'I don't think we should camp on somebody's tomb.'

'Well, what harm would it do?' said Hex.

Amber shrugged. 'We're going to eat, drink, sleep and – er – do other things here. It doesn't seem very respectful. It makes me really cross when people in the US put trailer parks on sacred Indian sites.'

Paulo started tracing the wall. It ran for some distance in a straight line. 'I don't think this is a tomb. More like some kind of agricultural terrace.' He came back and eased his bergen off. 'There's probably nothing sacred about it.'

Hex took his bergen off too. It was a relief to put it down – and let the air get to the sweaty patch of material underneath it. 'Who are these Maya anyway?'

Paulo swung his arms to loosen his shoulders. 'Lovely people. They lived in central America a few hundred years ago and were good at art, pyramids and bloody sacrifices.'

'Damn,' said Hex. 'We forgot to appease them by throwing a sacrifice into their pool. They'll hate us.'

Amber reluctantly took her bergen off too. She didn't look happy. She glared at Hex. 'You mean you don't know who the Maya Indians are? You must at least have seen them in a computer game.'

Hex swiftly moved up behind her, grabbed her and made his hand into an imaginary knife at her throat. 'Better than games,' he hissed menacingly, 'let's appease the gods right now.'

Amber shook free. 'Get off me, you nerdy creep.'

Alex saw her discomfort. 'Amber, I'm sure that's not a tomb. I think they're a bit taller than that.'

'Yes,' chipped in Hex. 'Pyramids, in fact.'

'Well, aren't you a mine of information?' said Amber. 'A moment ago you didn't know a Maya from a moron.' But she did look a bit happier.

'How long until dark?' asked Paulo.

'About an hour,' said Alex.

They got to work. Having stacked their bergens neatly, they enlarged the clearing by hacking down the undergrowth. Paulo used the machete and Alex used the hunting knife he carried at his belt. They each found a pair of trees for their hammock and put up green nylon ponchos – waterproof sheets, to act as a roof. In no time the small jungle clearing looked like a proper camp – the hammocks in a circle, each with a bergen beside it and a mosquito net. A small fire in the middle threw up a plume of smoke.

Alex was tying a piece of string to one of his hammock straps. He'd done the other ones already. 'Hey, guys, you should do this.'

'Why?' said Paulo.

'In case it rains. The water will run down the string. Otherwise it runs down the straps and makes a nice pool under your backside.'

They took off their wet clothes. Underneath they wore black lycra shorts to minimize rubbing from the constant sweating. Li and Amber had lycra sports tops too.

Li shed her shirt and trousers with visible relief. 'Yuck. I don't think I've ever been so filthy.' She put her black jungle boots upside down on sticks to stop wildlife getting into them and then put her clothes on hangers made from twigs.

Alex laughed. 'There's no point hanging those up. They'll never dry.'

'Is that the voice of Belize SAS experience I hear?' teased Amber.

'I don't care if they don't dry,' said Li. 'I feel better if I try.'

'Leech check,' said Paulo, walking up behind her. He carried a smouldering stick from the fire. Li stood still while he inspected her back and legs. A fat black leech was attached to her calf, pulsing as it sucked her blood. 'Yes, you've got a nice big one here.' He touched the smouldering stick to the leech. It shrank away from the heat and dropped to the floor. 'OK, you're clear. Who's next?'

Amber came forward for inspection. Paulo gave her the all clear and moved on to Hex.

'Oh lovely,' said Paulo. 'That one's huge. Hold still.'

Hex grimaced as he felt the heat of the smouldering stick near his skin. Then he felt Paulo clap him on his bare shoulder. 'All done.'

Hex glanced over his shoulder. The leech was on the ground, curling and wriggling. 'That's huge. How did that get in?'

Alex was next for inspection. 'Through your boots. See those eyelets?'

Amber was rubbing her legs with antiseptic wipes, cleaning the scratches she'd got from the wait-a-while. She looked at her jungle boot hanging on its stick. The hole was tiny, barely bigger than the hole in a sheet of Filofax paper, but the glistening, pulsing thing Paulo had removed from Hex was like a fat sausage. She looked at Alex. 'How?'

'They're like threads,' explained Alex. 'They swell up once they've had your blood. You also have to look out for little red crabs, like spiders. They bury their claws in your skin and feed on it. Some people get them more than others.'

'Alex,' said Paulo behind him, 'did your dad say he got them a lot? You're covered in them.'

Amber put antiseptic cream on her legs. She'd got a bite too; probably a mosquito. You had to take extra care with any wounds in the jungle. The hot, humid conditions meant that infections spread like wildfire – and with her diabetes she had to be especially careful as cuts might not heal as quickly as normal. When she'd finished she waved the medical pack in the air. 'Who's next for wound treatment?'

Li settled on her hammock with her boil-in-the-bag ration pack and dug her spoon in. It was something wet and meaty in a foil wrapper – not what she'd imagined as jungle fare – but it was hot and she was hungry. She shivered as the heat penetrated her hands. She hadn't realized how cold it would be at night.

They'd cleaned their wounds, put on insect repellent and were now in dry kit – a spare set of clothes
they'd brought for eating and sleeping in so that
they didn't have to stay in the sweat-sodden ones
they had worn all day. But the evening meal wasn't
a big comforting stew in a large pot around the fire.
They couldn't carry any large utensils, just a tiny
personal gas stove each. Cooking consisted of boiling
a mug of water and dunking a rations pack in it to
warm – although later on they planned to catch
local game and roast it, as they couldn't carry enough
rations packs for the whole trip. For now, though,
the fire in the middle of the camp was for light, heat
and to keep insects away.

Hex swallowed a spoonful of food and grimaced.
'What *is* this?' He lifted the pack and looked at the
label. 'English beef stew,' he read. 'They must have
searched every school kitchen in the land to come
up with something as bad as this.'

Alex dipped a spoon in but before he'd even
brought it to his mouth he wrinkled his nose. He
reached into his bergen, pulled out a tube of curry
paste and squeezed a dollop in.

Amber was watching him. 'Dad's advice?'

Alex nodded, his mouth chewing.

Amber looked down at her rations pack with distaste. 'Have you got any of that stuff to spare?'

Alex tossed the tube to her.

She caught it one-handed, squeezed some in and took a mouthful. She swallowed and nodded enthusiastically. 'Those SAS guys really are masters of survival. Anyone else?'

For a while it was nice to concentrate on eating. Trekking through the jungle had been physically and mentally exhausting, and now the camp was made they were looking forward to sleeping. They hadn't realized how dark it was getting until the dusk chorus started and the trees came alive with noise. Quails, hawks, toucans, parrots, guans, wrens, honeyleggers, motmots, iguanas, howler monkeys, spider monkeys, coatimundi, tapirs, peccaries, deer, ocelots and all sorts of insect – all of them called, chirped and howled as the sun slid down for the night.

When they started eating, the camp was shadowy, with chinks of light visible through the canopy. As they crumpled up the empty foil bags the darkness behind the trees was total and the only light was from the flickering fire.

Hex reached for his bergen and drew out a dark leather case. It contained a leather harness with straps and a device that looked like a pair of binoculars.

'Ah,' said Amber, making tea with the hot water she'd heated her rations pack in. 'Our homework.' It was a set of infra-red goggles for seeing in the dark – and the second element of their mission. The manufacturer, who knew her uncle, needed them tested to see how they stood up to the jungle humidity.

Hex slipped the harness plus goggles over his head.

Li, sipping a cup of tea, spluttered. He looked like someone with a couple of tubes strapped to his head, trying to be an alien. His dark hair stuck up in tufts between the straps of the headpiece.

'*Dios*,' said Paulo, 'you look like a bounty hunter from *Star Wars*.'

'It's not a good look without a helmet,' giggled Amber.

'I've never seen anything so ridiculous,' said Alex.

Hex hardly heard their remarks; he was far too intent on seeing what would happen when he switched on. And it certainly was different.

The darkness suddenly became see-through like gauze. The jungle was vast – greyish green and full of glowing white moving things. Small creatures scurried through the trees like mice; larger ones slunk after them, flashing in and out of view like lights as they passed behind grey foliage. Sleeping birds roosted next to dozing lizards. Snakes coiled like shadows around branches, their images dim and sinister as they watched the brighter warm-blooded creatures around them.

Hex looked at his four friends sitting in their hammocks. Their hands and faces were bright white, their bodies more shadowy where they were covered with clothes. There was Paulo's hair, wild, curly and white as though someone had unpinned the curls of a judge's wig. Amber's ebony skin was the same intense white as everyone else's. It made her look like a different person. Li's long plait faded into her clothes and looked like a scarf. Only Alex looked about the same as always.

Hex looked at the fire and the image flared with the intense heat. The jungle floor was teeming with life. Hex pulled his legs up sharply onto the hammock. Spiders scuttled across the ground, fat white blobs on spindly legs. Centipedes and millipedes were everywhere. He lifted the goggles away from his eyes. Everything was black and the ground next to the flickering fire looked as clear as if it had been swept. He put them on again. It was like an alternate universe. All those long spiky centipedes moving with a strange flowing motion, the tiny dots of smaller insects darting around.

'Hex,' said a voice sternly. An American voice. 'It's someone else's turn.'

'There's a centipede going up your trouser leg,' replied Hex.

In a millisecond Amber was out of her hammock, stamping furiously. 'Which leg?'

Hex grinned. There wasn't actually anything there but she didn't know that. 'Left.'

Amber shook her left foot vigorously, her mouth and eyes wide and worried. 'Has it gone?'

'I mean your right. I forgot, I'm looking at you.'

Amber stopped shaking her leg. Hex didn't make mistakes like that. He was having her on.

Hex saw Amber's head tilt to one side in an expression that was so familiar. Her baleful glare looked particularly malevolent through the goggles. 'By the way,' he said, 'you're as white as a sheet.' He handed the goggles to her with a grin.

Amber took them and put them on. She saw the alternate universe of busy insects and wished she hadn't. She took them off. 'Anyone else?'

Li stretched her hand out. 'Yes please. I want to know what I'm sharing my bedroom with.'

Paulo ran his fingers through his hair and gave her a macho look. 'Tell me, do I look as handsome in infra red?'

Li looked at Paulo through the goggles. 'Just big and hairy.'

He put his tongue out; the inside of his mouth glowed like a white-hot furnace.

She pointed the goggles towards the floor and saw what Hex had seen. White bodies scurried everywhere – crabs, millipedes, centipedes, tarantulas.

Alex, lying in his hammock, tucked up in his

sleeping bag, heard Li call his name. 'Mm?' he replied.

'You're covered in those little crabs,' she said.

Alex felt so sleepy. The hammock and sleeping bag enveloped him like a cocoon and his bones felt like lead. 'They're keeping me warm,' he said.

'They're even in your hair. It looks like you're wearing a veil.'

'Hmm,' said Alex. It was so blissful to be in the hammock, he didn't care.

He heard yawning and the others getting into their sleeping bags; Hex putting the goggles away. Alex imagined him tucking them back in their case lovingly.

Normally if they were sleeping somewhere strange they would set up a watch rota. But in the jungle only the animals moved at night, and the worrying ones lived close to the ground. Alex looked forward to eight hours' uninterrupted sleep.

A scream. Alex was instantly awake, panting in the darkness, listening. Had he really heard that? Had he dreamed it?

It came again. A dreadful scream. It went through to his marrow like a saw. What was it? Human? Animal? He groped for his torch and flicked it on.

Another torch beam flicked on at the same moment. Then the other three. The beams played around the camp area like nervous searchlights. Alex flinched as one caught his eyes.

'Is everyone OK?' He wasn't sure who shouted it but there were four replies of 'Yes'.

Still the noise went on. The scream was full of pain and fear. Again and again, like the crying of an inhuman child.

Paulo was sitting up. 'Li, are there jaguars in the jungle?'

'Yes,' she said. 'But they eat small things.' She was panting, trying to control herself after the fright.

'Well, that sounds like a big thing,' said Hex.

'But it's quite a long way off,' said Li.

'Hex,' suggested Amber, 'get those goggles.'

Hex was already rooting in his bergen. 'Believe me, I'm getting them.' He pulled the goggles out of their case and put them on.

As before, it was like a black curtain had dissolved.

Small white creatures were scuttling along on the ground; bigger animals were scurrying through the branches or looking around wide-eyed, startled by terrible noise. 'Nothing here.' He took the goggles off. The blackness descended again. He stowed the goggles in his bergen and got back into his hammock. 'Whatever it is, I don't think it's close,' he said.

'*Dios!*'

'What's that!'

'What the—?'

A sound of wood splintering. Crashing. Like something moving.

'It's being chased,' said Hex.

They listened, their hearts in their mouths. Was it coming closer? No, it just seemed random; like something going mad. And still it screamed.

'What if it comes this way?' Paulo asked.

'The fire will keep it away,' replied Alex.

They lay there, torches still on. It was like the terrible screaming thing was trying to break out of something. Break out of what?

Alex turned his torch off. 'I think we should try to go back to sleep. I don't think it will come near us.'

'If it does, I'll show it what a real scream is like,' said Amber.

Everyone laughed. That felt a bit better.

One by one, the other torches went off. Still the creature screamed and thrashed. Alex was wide awake to every sound and could hear the others moving restlessly, the trees creaking as they turned over in their hammocks. His heart was pounding as though he had been running. He turned over and then back again, trying to settle.

He must have been awake for ages before the noises began to subside. The crashing stopped. The scream became less constant, as though the creature was running out of breath. Gradually, as the five friends drifted into sleep, its cries died away.

4 DESTRUCTION

For a moment Alex thought he'd woken up on the moors. It was dark. The air was misty and dank, like a wet morning in Northumberland. Then the dawn chorus started. Not the polite chirrups of a few thrushes and sparrows greeting the day, but a full-throated, deafening rabble of jungle creatures up in the canopy as the sun rose.

Alex squirmed out of his sleeping bag and shivered. As he got out of his hammock, he saw Paulo sitting up, rubbing sleep out of his eyes. Amber was already on her feet, bent over, injecting her insulin.

Hex was checking that his palmtop was still in its protective carrying case – a reflex action on waking. Alex smiled at the sight and then found he'd just checked he had his survival kit and knife. Maybe Hex wasn't so strange after all.

Alex filled his cup with water from the sterilized supply. Hex was next to him and he handed over the container. Hex's face was grim. 'This bloody noise,' he said through gritted teeth, before stomping away to boil water on his little stove for breakfast. But Alex was enjoying the dawn chorus. It certainly beat waking to the breakfast show.

'Aaaargh.'

Alex looked round to see Amber hopping about on one leg as though she'd trodden on a spike. The other leg was thrust into her camouflage trousers. The fabric was soaking wet and clung to her skin.

'What's up?' said Alex.

'It's slimy, and clammy, and gritty—' She took a deep breath and put the other leg in roughly, pulled them up and fastened the waistband quickly, then did a vigorous jogging war dance to warm them up. 'Urgh, that is disgusting.'

Hex dunked his rations pack in his mug and smiled. 'That's why it's called wet kit.' Then he put his shirt on and his smile disappeared.

Li pulled on her wet shirt and trousers as quickly as she could, then launched into an explosion of karate kicks, trying to get warm.

Alex had got his shirt and trousers on with gritted teeth. Now he was psyching himself up for a very wet sock. He turned it inside out and found a glistening leech clinging to the material.

Paulo shrugged his wet shirt onto his bare back. Amber and Hex watched him, waiting for the reaction. He didn't even flinch. Not a flicker. They looked at each other, amazed.

Li came up behind them, still jogging on the spot, as Paulo pulled his trousers on, taking his time as though they were perfectly comfortable. She was rubbing her wet socks together in her hands, trying to warm them. 'Wet, dry, smelly – he simply doesn't notice, does he?'

She wasn't just talking about the wet kit. At times they'd had to go undercover in slums and Paulo had happily put on putrid rags, stiff with filth.

Paulo leaned over, inspected a wet sock and put his bare toes into it without a murmur. Silently, Amber and Hex shook their heads again.

Everything went back into their bergens: hammock, ropes, poncho, stove and dry kit were all carefully packed to stop water getting in. They refilled their water bottles and put away the collapsible storage containers.

Then it was the same routine: Paulo in the lead, same order behind. Count ten metres, check map, adjust position if necessary, move on.

Amber noticed Alex's face as they got back into the rhythm. 'You're still loving this, aren't you?'

Alex nodded.

'Glad somebody is.' Amber shivered. Normally she'd get warm if she was walking but they weren't able to move fast enough to do that, and the constant stopping was frustrating. Not only that, but her bite and the wounds from the wait-a-while plant were sore. She'd put more antiseptic on but the infection had taken hold. She'd just have to keep putting the cream on. Six more days of this began to seem like a very long time.

'You know what?' said Hex. 'I've come up with this theory for surviving the jungle. Don't go near it.' The camp had been an escape; now once again he was battling the nagging branches, the leaves in his face and the feeling that he was constantly squeezing through a gap that was a bit too small.

'What on earth was that thing screaming last night?' said Paulo. 'I've never heard anything like it.'

'Sounded vicious, whatever it was,' grumbled Hex. 'Li, how big is a jaguar?'

'Not very big,' replied Li. 'About the size of a dog.'

'What kind of dog?' said Amber. 'A poodle or a St Bernard?'

Alex looked thoughtful. 'Dad said some of the Indians talk about a creature that hunts the jaguar but I think it's a myth. Dad never saw it.'

'Well, did your dad ever hear anything like that screaming thing?' rejoined Paulo.

The others laughed nervously.

'Hey,' said Hex, 'did anyone ever see that film *Predator*, where there's an alien hunting people in the jungle?'

Paulo stopped. He'd seen something. 'Guys, look at this – it's been cleared.'

'It's a camp,' said Alex.

'A camp?' repeated Amber. 'Who else would be out here?'

An area about ten metres wide had been cleared, the foliage trodden down, and the ashy remains of a fire smouldered in the middle. One A-frame bed, made from local wood and lashed together with vines, stood in front of the fire area.

'It's a wrecked camp, to be precise,' said Hex. He pointed to the bed. One of its legs was shattered. The whole structure was tipped onto the floor. A cooking pot lay upside down near the fire. On the other side of the hearth was a frame of dampened woven branches, built to reflect heat like the back plate of a fireplace. One half had disintegrated entirely, its pieces scattered across the area.

The five friends looked at the destruction and the sweat running down their backs turned icy cold. Was this what they'd heard the previous night?

Amber's voice was a hoarse whisper. 'We were just

lying in our hammocks, totally vulnerable. What if it had come for us too?'

'It was quite a long way away,' said Li. But she sounded worried, not comforted.

Hex looked at the upturned cooking pot, the smashed bed. 'I thought things kept away if you had a fire.'

'So did I,' said Li quietly.

Paulo made a notch in a tree so they could deviate off course and investigate.

Alex and Hex squatted down to get a closer look at the debris in the fire area. On the ground was a fresh skin from a tapir. A couple of older animal skins lay stiff as cardboard in the leaf litter. Cigarette butts were sprinkled everywhere. And the whole lot looked like something had been dragged through it. 'Looks like someone was here for quite a while,' said Hex.

'Who'd be living out here?' asked Amber.

Alex replied, 'I suppose you always get someone living off the land, wherever you are.' With his finger he traced the tracks on the ground.

Hex stood up and dusted down his hands. 'But

he had a visitor. What on earth did this? A jaguar?'

Li was inspecting the bed frame. 'I don't see any blood. It doesn't look like he was dragged away. I think if it was a big cat there would have been some injuries – and claw marks on the wood.'

'Anyway, think of the noises we heard,' said Amber. 'Big cats sound like – well – big cats. Growling and stuff.'

Paulo was looking at the smashed fire screen. Nearby there were long marks raked through the leaf litter into the dark earth. It was like looking at a fence after a bull had broken out. 'Whatever it was, it was strong.'

The tracks went from the fire screen, past the bed frame and into the uncleared jungle, leaving a swathe of broken saplings and flattened vegetation.

'We've got ourselves a trail,' said Alex.

He and Paulo stepped into the undergrowth.

'How far are you going to go?' said Li.

Alex called back to her, 'We'll just take a quick look.'

Amber turned to Hex as she watched them follow the trail of wreckage. 'What if they find a body?'

Hex grimaced. 'What if they don't? There might not be anything left.'

Amber shuddered.

It wasn't long before Paulo's voice came back through the trees. 'Guys, come and look.'

Li led the way through the undergrowth. Paulo and Alex were standing looking at something on the ground. Alex was waving flies away from his face. An awful lot of flies.

'Do I really want to see this?' groaned Amber. 'What have you found?' She kept her eyes on Paulo and Alex until the last moment and then looked down.

'A donkey!' Li was incredulous.

It was lying on its side. Flies buzzed around its eye and nostril, packed into its ears like currants. They swarmed into various small wounds on its body.

'Probably died last night, by the look of it,' said Paulo.

'What killed it?' asked Hex. 'What are all those cuts?'

'It's not those you need to look at,' said Paulo. He touched his boot to the donkey's knee. A cluster of flies rose, buzzing angrily. Underneath was a swelling and a small, sticky wound. 'That's not like the other wounds. It's a snake bite. And look at this.' Paulo touched its head gently with his boot. The flies lifted; underneath was a dirty halter. There were sweat marks on its coat where it had carried panniers. 'It was probably tethered in the camp, got bitten, panicked and bolted.'

For a moment they looked down at the corpse. It looked so small and harmless. Big furry ears, its eyes and muzzle ringed with white fur. Poor thing, they thought, to die like that.

They retraced their steps back through the camp to the notch in the tree. Amber and Alex reorientated themselves with the map and they were soon back into their routine again.

'A donkey,' said Hex. He began to giggle. He tried not to but it quivered inside him like jelly. Next to him, he saw Amber's eyes and mouth screw up.

That was it. The five friends roared helplessly, clutching each other, holding trees, letting out the tension.

Li was the first to recover. 'It's not funny.' She

dabbed her eyes, shaking her head. 'It must have been horrible.'

'We really scared ourselves there,' gasped Amber. She caught Hex's eye.

'A donkey,' he said severely.

Amber biffed him on the shoulder. 'Oh, don't make me laugh again – it hurts.' But then she was off again, and so were the others.

She stopped laughing all of a sudden and froze.

'Hey, Amber,' said Hex, 'why so serious?'

Amber spoke through gritted teeth. 'There's something under my foot.' Slowly she looked down.

The others followed her gaze.

The last embers of their laughter dwindled away when they saw what it was.

Just beyond the black toe of Amber's boot something in the shape of an arrowhead was swaying from side to side.

A snake.

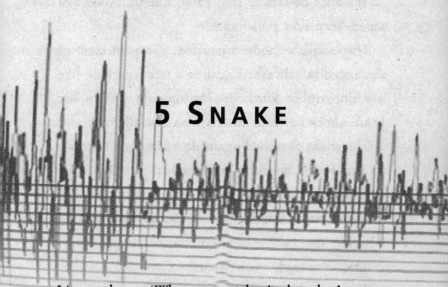

5 SNAKE

Li moved away. 'Whatever you do, Amber, don't move. Your foot is stopping it biting. Alex, you're too close.'

Alex shifted backwards, never taking his eyes off the thing Amber was standing on. She had her boot on it, just behind its head. The rest of its body lay in a coil behind her. It blended so well with the dark brown leaf litter that until it moved it was invisible.

Amber stared down. She felt it shift under her boot and froze. Her stomach did a somersault. 'Um . . . the way you're all looking at it tells me it might be a bit . . . poisonous?'

'It's a fer-de-lance,' said Paulo quietly. 'A kind of viper. Very, very poisonous.'

The snake's body uncurled. Two metres of zigzagged tail thrashed against a tree, cracking like a whip. Amber flinched. One thought was in her head – keep her foot where it was, at all costs.

The snake thrashed again. It was angry. Hex felt its tail touch his foot and crashed into Li as he darted away.

Amber took deep breaths. It was like standing on a mine – one false move and someone could die.

'OK,' she said. 'Now what?'

'We all run away and you stay standing there,' said Hex. 'Only joking.'

'That's not funny.'

'How does she get her foot off the snake?' asked Alex. 'Should she just take it off and run?'

Li shook her head. 'They can move lightning fast. She might outrun it, but if she doesn't we're a hell of a long way from a hospital.'

Amber had a flashback to the night before: the donkey's screams. It had gone on for hours. That was how long it had taken to die.

'We'll have to kill it,' said Hex. 'Paulo, you've got a machete. Cut its head off.'

'I might chop Amber's foot off at the same time,' said Paulo.

'We could club it to death,' said Alex.

Paulo was shaking his head. 'We don't have to kill it.'

Amber snorted. 'Thanks. You can afford to be all fluffy. You haven't got your foot on it.'

'On the ranch we'd kill it,' replied Paulo, 'but that's domesticated land. This is wild. We shouldn't try to turn it into our backyard.' He hefted the machete. The snake registered his movement and lifted its head, giving him a flash of yellow throat.

'Careful,' snapped Amber. A shaft of sunlight filtering through the trees glinted off Paulo's blade. Her eyes widened even further. 'What are you going to do?'

'Give us a head start.' Paulo sliced a thin branch off a nearby tree and chopped it so that it ended in a fork, three centimetres across.

'He's got a plan,' said Li. 'He's got that look on his face.' The Argentinian loved tinkering with machines

– or making them out of whatever materials he had to hand.

Paulo passed the branch to Amber. 'Do you think this will go over the neck of the snake?'

She lowered the branch until it was near the snake. It reared its head up and tried to strike. The movement was so violent it actually made her ankle wobble. 'Vicious little beggar,' muttered Amber and pulled the stick back sharply. She passed it to Paulo. 'It'll probably fit.'

Paulo gave the stick to Alex. 'Can you sharpen the ends so they'll stick into the ground, first go?'

Alex took the stick and began to pare it with his hunting knife. 'Spill the beans, Paulo, what are you making?'

'I think I know,' said Hex. 'Amber will put that stick over the snake's head, where her foot is. It will be stuck and we can go.'

'With one modification,' said Paulo. 'We'll have to let it go. Otherwise we're just leaving it in a trap.'

'It we let it go it'll chase us,' said Hex.

'But we can get a head start, then pull the stake out with a length of vine.' Paulo handed the machete to Li. 'I need it as long as you can get.'

She cut a piece of vine and began to pull out a length of it. It was strong, like cord. She began to make a coil of it around her arm like a cable.

Amber realized her legs were burning. The wait-a-while cuts had chosen this moment to flare up. She looked down at them, longing to dig her nails in and give them a good scratch. 'You just take your time, guys,' she said. 'I've got these cuts that are itching like hell, but I can hang on.'

Alex handed the sharpened stick back to Paulo. 'You shouldn't scratch anyway. You'll make them worse.'

'Yes, thanks for the sermon,' grumbled Amber.

Li handed Paulo the vine. He looked at it and did a rough calculation of how much there was.

Hex watched him. 'Paulo, when this contraption of yours is all in place, are we going to stroll away or run like hell?'

'We've got about four metres of vine. That's not a huge head start. We'll still have to run.'

'In that case,' said Hex, 'a few of us should get ahead now and mark the way. Then you wait a bit before releasing the snake and—'

Amber glared at him. 'Are you trying to wind me up? You want me to wait like this even longer?'

Hex shrugged. 'We've spent all this time trying not to get lost. Pity to throw it all away.'

'Hex is right,' said Alex. 'I don't mind staying behind.'

Paulo tied one end of the vine onto the forked stick. 'No, I'll stay.' He pulled the knots to test them. 'After all, this is my contraption.' He handed Alex the machete. 'We'll catch you up.'

Alex got his map out of his belt kit. It took just moments to reorientate himself. He looked at Hex and Li. 'Ready?'

They nodded. Hex looked back at Amber. 'Make sure you nail the squirmy little beggar firmly into the ground.'

'I'll get him, don't you worry,' said Amber. She wished she felt as confident as she sounded.

Hex and Li headed off after Alex, counting paces. Amber's heart thudded in time with their feet crunching on the leaf litter. Hex trod on a branch and the crack flooded her brain with images: the crashes and the screams in the night, the trail of destruction as the poor, panicking donkey tried to escape the pain of the snake bite.

Paulo coiled up the free end of the vine and stood behind her. He handed her the stick. 'Just slide it into the ground, in front of where you've got your foot. Make sure it's firm.'

Amber took the stick. 'If it doesn't work, do I get my money back?' She positioned it behind the snake's head. It reared back, eyes watching her like black sequins. She rammed the stick into the ground hard and it slid in like a garden fork.

Paulo gave a tug on the vine.

'Don't do that!' hissed Amber.

'Just testing. Now take your foot away.'

'Are you sure?'

Paulo nodded. 'It's held securely.'

Very slowly, Amber raised her foot a millimetre. The snake felt the pressure release and humped its back. Amber froze.

'Keep going,' said Paulo. 'Its head is still pinned.'

Sweat was running down Amber's face. She held onto Paulo and slowly lifted her foot. She looked down. The snake was held firmly by the stick, as though it had been stapled into the ground.

Paulo took her arm and moved her away. 'Now we follow the others.'

The snake hissed at them, showing pale fangs. It knew they were moving.

Amber couldn't take her eyes off it. 'What if it slides out?'

'It can't. It's a close fit.'

Amber turned round. The others had vanished but they were easy to follow thanks to the path Alex had cut with the machete. Behind her, Paulo paid out the vine, looking backwards all the time. If it got caught, it might release the snake before they had got far enough away.

Li's voice sang through the trees. 'Are you there?'

Amber called back. 'We're coming. Go on ahead.'

Paulo continued to pay out the line. 'We're nearly at the end. Ready to run?'

'Sure.'

'Go!' As Paulo started to run he felt the vine snag and pull free. The snake was released.

'Go go go!' he yelled.

Amber ran. Demons pursued her, images of what

would happen if she didn't run fast enough. Her bergen thumped on her back, pushing her on. Eventually, Paulo, Hex, Li and Alex closed in around her, pulling her back, telling her she could stop.

She collapsed in a heap on the jungle floor, getting her breath. 'Has it gone?' she gasped.

Paulo was nodding. 'Yes. It's gone.'

Amber pulled herself up onto all fours, still breathing heavily. She looked up at Alex. 'Can we just do some boring navigation for a while now? After all, that's what we came for.'

Paulo in front, Alex and Amber next, Hex and Li at the back. Every ten metres, stop and check. They felt they were getting better at this. They slipped into the routine more easily, each playing their part like components in a machine. It was repetitive, but now they were all working so well together there was something satisfying about it.

'Hey,' said Paulo, 'there are some more of these drystone walls.'

Alex bent down and brushed aside some of the vines. The stones formed a mound, sloping away from him into the undergrowth. 'No, they're different. Look.'

The others stopped and looked. The mound was at least as tall as Alex was.

Alex knew what it was. His dad had described them. 'That,' he said, 'is a pyramid. A tomb.'

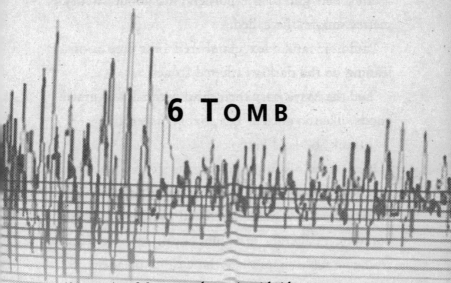

6 TOMB

'A genuine Maya tomb . . .' said Alex.

'It's almost completely hidden,' said Hex. 'We could be the first to find it.'

While Paulo marked a notch on a tree, Amber started to trace the perimeter, stepping high to avoid the brambles and wait-a-while. 'It's quite big.' She walked further along and then stopped. 'I can see the corner.'

'Hang on,' said Alex. 'Don't go out of sight.'

'Let's look at the other side,' said Li. 'Come on, guys.'

Alex had got to the corner. 'It's about twenty metres square,' he called.

Paulo, Li and Hex clambered over tree roots, leaning on the dark weathered stones.

'Did the Maya bury their dead with a lot of grave goods, like the ancient Egyptians?' asked Li.

'I think so,' said Paulo.

Hex traced his fingers along the stones. One row had been carved, like a stripe of patterned tiles in a bathroom. They were weathered back to shadows but were deliberate markings: ovals, dots, circles; strange bubble shapes like the writing of aliens.

They heard Amber's voice. 'Hey, guys. This is the entrance.'

They hurried along to the end of the wall. Alex and Amber were standing by a tall black opening, tapered at the top, made of big stone slabs. It faced into a wooded valley.

Hex looked at Amber. 'OK, we've finished here. Let's be respectful and leave the tomb in peace.'

Amber was too excited to rise to his sarcasm. 'I don't think it's disrespectful to investigate,' she smiled. 'After all, this could be preserved for the nation.' She got out her torch and flashed it into the opening. The light bounced off mud-coloured stones.

The others got their torches out too. Hex angled his downwards. 'Hey, guys, there are steps.'

Four torch beams converged on Hex's. They revealed a perfectly preserved set of stone steps going down into the darkness.

Paulo swept his torch over the walls. 'I can't see the bottom. Looks like it goes down for quite a way.'

Alex slipped off his bergen and propped it against the tomb wall. 'Who's coming exploring?'

'Doesn't look like there's room for more than one at a time,' said Li. 'Why don't you go down and see what's there? It might be blocked.'

'Hey,' said Hex. He took off his bergen and pulled out the night vision goggles. 'Take these. You'll get a better view.'

Alex put the strap over his shoulder. 'Thanks.' He stepped into the opening.

Paulo played a torch on Alex's back to keep an eye on him. The steps went down sharply and soon all they could see was the top of his blond head.

Paulo looked at the others and grinned. 'Following in Dad's footsteps.'

Hex shuddered as he watched Alex descend. The tunnel came to a blunt point at the top, like a coffin. Alex seemed to be heading into inky blackness. Rather him than me, thought Hex.

Alex took it slowly. The steps were steep, as though they were made by a race of people with longer legs than normal. It was hot; the rocks caught the sweat coming off him and held it. It was damp and smelled of animal droppings, like a cave.

A few more steps and he would be at the bottom. Alex stopped and listened. It sounded as though something was moving down there. A noise like something crunching around on gravel. Was it an animal? Certainly enough wildlife had been in and out recently. There could be something living down there. He turned the torch downwards.

Something threw him against the wall of the tunnel. He gasped and the sound was magnified by the close walls. He steadied himself. He was sure he hadn't tripped. It was like he'd been hit but he hadn't felt a blow – anyway there was no one else there. Yet his shoulder was singing with pain where a bruise was forming.

It happened again. This time he was thrown forwards and his hands ground into the gritty guano on the steps.

Amber's voice shrieked down to him. 'Alex get out, it's a quake!'

There was a rumbling noise like the deepest notes on a cathedral organ. Alex powered up the steps. Stones and crusts of ancient bird droppings fell around him. He burst into the daylight. Paulo and Hex grabbed him and pulled him away from the tomb. The earth was shaking and they dived to the ground, covering their heads with their arms. A tree crashed over.

The quake stopped. For a long moment the five friends didn't dare move.

'Are we still alive?' Hex's voice was shaky.

Alex sat up. 'Everyone all right?'

'Hex, get off my foot,' said Amber. 'Then I'll be all right.'

Some trees close by had fallen, but the damage to the tomb looked worse. The outer stones from one corner had tumbled away, showing pale surfaces.

'Lucky you got out,' said Amber.

Alex patted his shoulder suddenly. 'Damn.'

'What?' said Paulo.

'I dropped the night vision goggles.'

Amber high-stepped back to the entrance and flashed her torch into the tunnel. There were the goggles. They looked a very long way down. 'I can see them.'

Hex came up behind her, followed by the others. 'It's all right, they're shock proof.'

Amber was talking fast, an edge of panic in her voice. 'Can we risk going down for them? We are in deep trouble if we lose them. I promised we were just going to do nice boring things like trekking, not exploring tombs. You know what my uncle's like. If we don't get them back in one piece . . .'

She didn't need to say any more. If John Middleton suspected how dangerous their 'holidays' really were he'd withdraw his support – and there would be no more Alpha Force.

Paulo began playing his torch over the walls. 'Let's see if it's safe to go back in.'

Alex was kicking himself. 'They must have slipped off my shoulder. I should have had them on more securely.'

Paulo clicked off his torch. 'The walls still look straight. I don't think anything structural has moved. I think it's safe to go down.'

Alex put his foot on the first step. 'Right, I'll be two ticks.' He went down into the tunnel, moving as fast as he dared.

He reached the goggles and put them carefully over his shoulder and across his body. Now they shouldn't fall off.

He had just started back up when he heard something. A desperate cry. It sounded human. He flashed the torch around behind him but he could only see walls. 'Hello?' he shouted. His voice echoed.

'Hello?' called Li's amused voice from far up above.

'Not you,' called Alex.

The noise came again. It was definitely down in the pyramid – and it sounded like a cry of pain.

Alex cupped his hand to his mouth and called up. 'There's someone down here. Get Paulo and the medical kit.'

In the tunnel opening he saw Paulo slip his bergen off. A moment later he was pattering down, his broad shoulders nearly obscuring the light. 'What's up?'

Alex flashed the torch down the remainder of the staircase. 'I think there's someone in here.'

Five steps and they reached the bottom. It was well beyond the point where daylight would penetrate. They flicked their torches around. It was a small space, with barely enough room for the two well-built teenagers to turn around without their belt packs catching on each other.

'It's just a dead end,' said Paulo.

'Hello?' called Alex. 'Where are you? We've come to help.'

There was no answer. 'There was definitely someone here,' he went on.

'Did your dad ever say how you get into these places?'

Alex shone his torch over the walls and looked at them carefully. 'No. I think he didn't want to give me ideas.'

'Aha.' Paulo had noticed something. Two of the walls were made of blocks, but the third looked a little different. 'Look, this is carved to look as though it's made of blocks, but it seems to be solid. Like a door.'

He pushed. It swung open noiselessly, as though on well-oiled hinges. 'Maya engineering,' whistled Paulo. 'Bueno.' He walked into the chamber. 'Hello?'

There was a click.

Alex rugger-tackled Paulo to the ground. There was a flash and a bang, and a piercing whistle as something ricocheted off the walls.

7 ROBBER

They heard Amber's voice from far away on the surface. 'Are you OK?'

Alex shouted back through the open door, 'Yes.'

A smell of cordite and gunpowder filled the tiny space. Paulo retrieved his torch and shone it around. A shotgun stood on the floor, its barrel propped up by rocks. A branch lay in front of them, vines linking it to the trigger. It must have been wedged in the door, ready to fall if it was opened. A booby trap. And it didn't look like it had been set by the ancient Maya.

Alex found his torch and went for the weapon. It was an old shotgun. Alex knew the type – it held just one round at a time, so it wasn't about to go off again. The wood was battered but the barrel wasn't rusty. It was a working, well-maintained weapon. He broke the breech and pulled out a spent red cartridge.

A voice babbled angrily from the darkness. Paulo swept the torch around the room. It met two glistening eyes at floor level, blinking back at him. Dense black hair, frosted with dust. Thick Indian lips revealing missing teeth. A sweat rag tied around the forehead.

'Hello,' said Paulo. 'Nice welcome. Do you speak English? *Espagnol?*'

The man looked at them blankly and then spoke a few words.

Alex looked at Paulo. 'Is that a Spanish dialect?'

Paulo shook his head. 'It's like nothing I've ever heard.' He flashed the torch over the man. He was lying next to what seemed to be a sarcophagus. A large flat slab of stone, about two metres long, had fallen onto the man's leg and pinned him to the floor.

'A tomb robber,' said Alex. 'It looks like he was trying to move that slab. He'd closed the door so he wouldn't be seen and rigged it so that if anyone came in they'd get shot. Then the earthquake hit.'

'Watch him,' said Paulo, 'while I check his injuries.' Although the robber probably couldn't hurt them, they weren't going to take their safety for granted after such a greeting. He certainly seemed to be looking at Paulo and Alex with hostility. 'I hope he hasn't got friends outside who'll come and sort us out.'

Alex leaned against a stone chest. It put him above the man's eye line. All the better to reinforce the idea that they were in control, just in case. 'No, I think he's working on his own. Otherwise why the booby trap?'

The robber glared at Alex, then flinched away from the bright torch. Alex kept the light on him for a little longer than he needed to. Being shot at made him a bit unsympathetic. The sarcophagus behind hardly seemed to be worth the bother anyway. From what Alex could see it contained only dusty skeletons of birds and a few pieces of pottery.

Paulo got to work. Years of tending injured animals on the ranch had made him a natural medic, and he'd been on courses since. First, was there any bleeding? No.

'Shall we move that slab?' asked Alex.

'Yes,' said Paulo. Then he changed his mind. 'No. Wait a minute. Let me think.' A little voice was telling him to be careful with crush injuries. Damaged muscles released toxic chemicals into the bloodstream. When you released the patient, these would flow out of the trapped limbs and could prove fatal. But Paulo had a feeling this case would be OK. Why? he asked himself. You couldn't go on a hunch when a man's life might be at stake. It came back to him. It would be all right because the injured man had been trapped for only a short time.

'Are we moving this thing or not?' said Alex.

'Yeah.' Paulo bent down and Alex went to the other side.

The man let out a cry as they took hold. 'It's OK,' said Paulo. 'We won't hurt you.'

'We don't bear grudges, after all,' added Alex.

They pushed. The slab was heavy but they managed

to lean it against the sarcophagus. The casualty struggled to sit up and fell back, panting.

Paulo looked at Alex, incredulous. 'Do you think he's trying to escape?'

'Well, I suppose he thinks we're going to put him in jail.'

Paulo knelt down next to him. 'Shh,' he said. 'Just hold still. Let's see what you've done.'

The right leg was an odd shape, with a bulge halfway down the thigh, just below a ragged pair of shorts. Paulo ran his torch up and down it. 'A few bumps and scrapes, but it's already stopped bleeding.' He was about to touch the swelling, but the man grabbed his hand, his eyes urgent.

Paulo pulled away. 'OK, I get it; that hurts.' The leg was probably broken. Even if the man could get free he couldn't go anywhere.

'Alex, can you call the heli?' said Paulo. 'He needs to go to hospital.'

'I'll get the others to build a stretcher,' Alex replied as he left the tomb.

Paulo sat back and thought about his patient. Was there anything else he needed to do? The man was breathing easily, if fast. He wasn't in shock, but of course that might happen at any minute. Paulo shone his torch on the man's foot. It was shoeless; the sole was like leather and the skin was filthy. But the toes were the same colour as those on the other foot and they weren't turning blue, so the blood supply wasn't damaged and the limb wasn't about to die. He seemed stable. Paulo relaxed a little.

As he got to his feet, something in the sarcophagus caught his eye. He shone the torch over it.

A face looked back at him – eyes, lips and skin covered in the centuries-old dust. He flicked the torch away, shocked. Was it a mummy?

He realized the robber was watching him closely. He'd already spotted what Paulo had seen. There was a possessive look in his eyes. What was in there?

Paulo slowly shone the torch back into the tomb.

It was a face, but it wasn't flesh. It was still and solid. Nor did it look like a skull; it looked like a piece of art.

Paulo reached into the tomb and brushed it gently with his fingers.

The man on the floor spoke rapidly in his incomprehensible language. He sounded angry.

Where Paulo's hand had been was a trail of bright gold.

Li came down the steps. 'Alex and the others are making a stretcher – I thought I'd come down and . . .' She tailed off. Paulo was staring down at something in his hands.

He saw her and turned it round so that she could see.

A mask of gold.

Li gasped. She moved towards it. Paulo handed it to her carefully. Made from beaten gold, the mask was a lifelike face with a wide forehead, aristocratic nose and fine lips. The eyes had small pupil-like holes, and between the parted lips was a T-shaped piece of silver.

'I thought it was a corpse when I saw it in there,' said Paulo. 'I saw that face and nearly ran out to join you guys.'

The man on the floor let out another tirade.

'Ignore him,' said Paulo. 'He's been grumbling ever since we arrived.'

Li shone her torch into the tomb. There was a skeleton, brown and looking as crumbled as old leaves. It wore a jade ring around its twig-like finger and big circles of jade positioned where each ear would have been. Around the edge of the sarcophagus were carvings.

There were footsteps outside and Alex came into the chamber. Hex and Amber followed behind, carrying the stretcher. They'd cut down saplings and threaded them through one of the hammocks.

They manoeuvred it into the small space while Paulo assessed the patient. 'I think we should splint the leg. Otherwise the broken ends of the bones are going to rub together when we move him.'

Hex glanced towards the door. 'Tell me what you need and I'll go and get it.' He sounded keen to get out.

'A piece of wood, like you used for the stretcher.' Paulo held his hands so that they were about a metre apart. 'About this long, or longer. Plus lots of bandages and something to pad the leg.'

'Sure.' Hex turned and was out in a flash.

Amber watched him as he bounded up towards

the sky. 'He didn't want to come down,' she said. 'He offered to stay on watch at the top. Only I told him there was nothing to watch.'

'Amber,' said Alex, 'sometimes you are a pure sadist.'

But Amber was shining her torch around the walls, curious to see her surroundings. Suddenly she gasped. 'Oh wow, what's all this?' Her beam found a detailed frieze in green and rusty red. It was one of the most beautiful things she had ever seen.

Alex ran up the stairs. The heli was due to fly overhead soon on its way to the rigs. If they were going to catch it today they had to set up the signal immediately.

He found his bergen and drew out a bag. Then he had to pick his spot. It didn't have to be somewhere the heli could land, but it did have to be under a gap in the tree canopy so they could communicate by hand signals. He found one just a few metres away.

He unpacked the signalling equipment. There was a large red balloon and a big rubberized bladder. Alex filled the bladder with water from their supplies, trying to keep the opening upright. It looked a bit disgusting, like a cow's udder. There was a sachet of chemicals, printed with warnings not to eat them. Alex tore the wrapper open and poured the powder into the water. When it hit the liquid it started fizzing. Good. Now he had to get the red balloon over the mouth of the bladder of water. He suspected it wouldn't be as easy as it sounded. In his experience balloons tended to squirm away at the crucial moment, especially from sweaty fingers. But to his surprise the balloon went onto the bladder easily.

The water was fizzing furiously and the bladder was warm. Whatever those chemicals were, they were producing a fierce reaction. The balloon was growing. He had visions of it pinging off the bladder and zooming into the trees with a rubbery fart. He secured the two together with a metal twist tie, taking no chances.

The balloon was now a metre wide. Alex took the last item out of the kit – a piece of cord. He tied one end around the neck of the balloon, tied the other around a secure branch and stood the whole thing on the ground, lined up with the gap in the trees. Now he didn't mind if it lifted off.

The balloon grew to two metres and began to rise. Alex grinned with triumph as it lifted past the trees, sending birds scattering in a flutter of wings and startled hoots. Soon the cord was taut, moving as the balloon drifted on air currents above. Alex remembered when they first arrived: the vast plain of green that was the tree canopy seen from above. Now there would be a big red blob in the middle of the green, tethered above their position.

Alex heard noises from the tomb. Amber came into view, walking backwards very slowly with the handles of the stretcher. Alex rushed to help but they seemed to have enough manpower. Paulo and Hex were at the other end, holding the stretcher on their shoulders like pallbearers so that they could get the awkward load up the stairs. Li brought up the rear, shining her torch so it lit the way for Paulo and Hex. In her other hand was the gold mask.

When Amber reached the surface Alex took one of the handles. Once Hex and Paulo were on level ground the four of them manoeuvred the stretcher onto one of the walls at the edge of the tomb and set it down gently. That way, it would be easier to lift again.

'Heli should be passing over soon,' said Alex.

Paulo drew a hand across his forehead, getting his breath back as he checked on the patient again. 'We'll have to check his circulation every twenty or thirty minutes. In case a blood vessel's been crushed.'

Hex shook his head to get rid of the drops of sweat dribbling down his forehead. 'We can use the infra-red goggles. It will show if his extremities are getting cold.' He slicked his fringe back and looked around. 'Where are they, by the way?'

Paulo suddenly felt rather alarmed. Alex had been wearing them when they'd crashed to the ground trying to avoid being shot. He handed the goggles to Hex without comment, but behind his back Paulo could see he had his fingers crossed.

Hex got the case open and powered the goggles up. He looked through them at the robber's legs. 'The patient looks fine.' He took the goggles off and put them away.

Li was carefully brushing the dust off the golden mask. It gleamed in the light that filtered down through the trees. The face was so lifelike she felt she could see what the dead man had really looked like, all those years ago.

Alex looked dubious. 'You decided to bring the mask out?'

'It belongs in a museum,' said Li. 'If we leave it here now the tomb's been opened, someone else might come along and help themselves.'

'Fair point,' Alex agreed.

'There was other stuff in there too,' said Amber. 'More jewellery.' She rolled up her trouser leg and scratched, ignoring Alex's disapproving look. 'Once we've dropped this guy off in hospital we can take it to the big museum in Belize City.'

Alex looked annoyed. 'Wait a minute. I didn't think we were going to Belize City. We've still got our exercise to do.'

Hex was looking at the mask. He felt its weight. It had to be solid gold. 'We've got to take it there in person,' he said. 'This thing must be priceless. It wouldn't be fair to just give it to the pilot, pat him on the back and say, "Drop that off, there's a good chap"?'

'Hex is right,' said Paulo. 'We've got to take it ourselves.'

Alex looked glum but had to agree. 'I suppose we can come back and pick up where we left off.'

'I'll tell you something else,' said Hex. 'We'd better get the other valuables that are in that tomb or they'll disappear.'

Amber jumped to her feet. 'Good idea. Are you coming?'

She was only teasing but Hex's shudder was for real. 'Not a chance.'

But Li was keen. She hurdled a wait-a-while plant and joined Amber. 'We should take some pictures of the friezes so we can show the archaeologists. Anyone got a camera phone?'

As she spoke there was a loud rumble followed by a crash. The trees shook, sending birds squealing into the sky.

The five friends froze in a shocked tableau: Hex wrapping the mask in cotton wool from the medical kit; Paulo at the stretcher, adjusting the robber's splint; Alex getting up off his bergen to go down into the tomb with Li and Amber.

Li swallowed nervously. 'Was that a quake?'

Amber moved cautiously towards the mouth of the tomb. 'Oh,' she said.

The other four went to join her.

One side of the tunnel that led down into the tomb had caved in.

'I think,' said Alex, 'we'd better leave the dangerous stuff to the archaeologists.'

The birds, barely settled again, suddenly took off in a squawking panic, bright feathers flashing through the green foliage. And there was another sound – the steady beat of rotors; the high whine of an engine. The helicopter was coming.

8 Landing Zone

They ran to the little clearing and looked up at the signal balloon. It was buffeted in the air currents like a punch bag. The bright sky hurt their eyes after the permanent twilight under the tree canopy; they felt like nocturnal animals as they squinted up into real daylight. The belly of the helicopter passed over, a black torpedo sliding through the sky. It circled away then hovered, the winch man at the open side door, looking down.

Alex waved. The winch man waved back. They had contact. Alex lay down flat on his back, his legs straight out and his arms stretched above his head. It was the international sign for 'casualty on a stretcher'.

Above him, the heli flew away and circled back again. As it passed the gap it did a wobbling movement, tipping its rotors from one side and then the other. Alex knew what that meant: *message understood*.

The heli came back and hovered. Soon a shape began to descend out of the aircraft, a strange black silhouette. As it came below the tree canopy the light changed and they realized what it was: two chainsaws, lashed together. All of them asked themselves the same question: why was the winch man sending down chainsaws?

Li leaned close to Paulo so he could hear her above the noise of the heli. 'Maybe you're supposed to cut the robber's leg off.'

He looked at her and shrugged, just as mystified.

The chainsaws were rustling through the lower leaves and heading for the ground. Hex went to grab one.

'Don't touch it!' yelled Paulo. 'You'll get an electric shock. Aircraft build up a lot of static electricity. Let the cable touch the ground first.'

Hex stopped where he was. 'Whoa,' he muttered to himself. 'That could really liven up my day.'

The chainsaws touched down and the rope went slack. Up above, more strange shapes were coming down on ropes. When they arrived they turned out to be fuel cans, two orange suits of protective chain-mail clothing and a metal box about the size of a shoebox.

Once everything was safely unloaded, Alex waved up at the winch man. The ropes snaked back up into the sky. The winch man gave a final wave and the heli moved away.

Once it had gone the jungle seemed strangely still and quiet.

'OK, Alex,' said Amber. 'I thought he was picking us up. Why has he gone away again? And what are all these toys for?'

'The pilot can't land to pick up the stretcher,' replied Alex. 'He wants us to cut a landing zone.'

Amber scratched her leg. The wait-a-while cuts were still really itchy and tender. She'd been hoping that if they went back to Belize City she could get some antibiotics. 'This jungle business just gets better,' she grumbled.

Paulo was also disappointed not to be getting in a helicopter immediately, but the thought of an engineering challenge perked him up. 'We want a flat area about thirty metres wide, with a firm surface. Not here,' he added. 'Those tombs won't cope with ten tonnes of helicopter landing on them.'

'We need to be on a ridge line,' said Alex. 'Then the trees will be easier to clear.'

Amber unfolded the map briskly and pointed. 'There's an ideal spot just there. About ten minutes' walk away.' She was keen to get moving. When she had a job to do the wait-a-while itching wasn't so bad.

Alex nodded. 'Yeah. Take someone and scout ahead; the rest of us can follow with the stretcher.'

She picked up both chainsaws and swung one over to Hex. 'Congratulations. You're my pacesetter.'

Hex barely caught it before she turned round and set off. 'See you in a bit, guys,' he said to the others.

As soon as Hex started walking behind her, he was counting paces. It seemed like second nature now; once he got back to civilization he probably wouldn't be able to stop himself doing it. It would be like a subroutine forever running in his head.

As Hex and Amber disappeared, Paulo did a quick check on the patient. Not having a common language he couldn't ask him how he was feeling, but he guessed the splint had made him more comfortable. Certainly his breathing was steadier. Paulo felt the man's toes. Both feet were the same temperature. So no circulation problems yet.

Meanwhile Alex cut the cord of the signal balloon with his knife. Another important rule of survival: never leave your distress markers once the call has been answered.

The free end of the rope drifted up. Li came and watched as the balloon caught a thermal and shrank until it was only a dot in the sky. 'Maybe we should have put a message on it: *Dear Mum and Dad, Having a super time . . .*'

The three prepared to follow the others, distributing the rest of the gear. Alex made a bee-line for the metal box. The others didn't notice the smile playing across his lips as he put it in his bergen. He was sure it was going to make clearing the landing zone an awful lot more fun.

* * *

Li and Paulo lowered the stretcher carefully to the ground so as not to jar the injured man's leg. Alex put down the fuel cans.

Hex was taking his bergen off. 'Do you want the good news first? No old Maya structures, so it should all be solid ground.'

Amber was standing next to a mahogany. 'But the bad news is we'll have to clear nearly twenty trees.' She thumped the trunk of the tree behind her. 'And that includes this monster.'

The tree was nearly three metres in diameter, with buttresses flaring out like a bell of fabric from the bottom. They looked around at the rest of the area. Many of the other trees were not as big, but they were solid oaks – at least a metre in diameter. It looked like hard work.

Paulo unloaded the protective chain mail off the stretcher. 'Alex, what's so funny?'

Alex was smiling as he slipped his bergen off. He opened the top and took out the metal box. 'I've almost been hoping we'd have a chance to do this.'

'Yeah,' said Amber. 'Somehow we can tell.'

'Don't tell me,' said Li. 'You've brought some wood lice.'

'Beavers?' suggested Hex.

Almost reverently, Alex opened the box and revealed the contents. It contained forty white sticks about the length of a Cumberland sausage, wrapped in cellophane. 'This,' he said, 'is plastic explosive. I went on a course at half term. Ladies and gentlemen, I am now qualified to blow holes in things.'

'I admit that's very cool,' said Li. 'But what good is it right now?'

Alex lifted the sticks of plastic explosive out of the box. Underneath were drilling tools and some other, smaller boxes. 'We put a couple of holes in each tree and stick some explosive in. Then – bang. Job done. We'll be back in Belize City in time for dinner. I don't think we're going to need those chainsaws.'

His words lifted the group's mood in an instant. It was though the sun had come out.

Amber felt her old positive self again. 'Hex has marked the trees we need to move. There's a cross on each of them.'

'That wasn't me,' said Hex, his voice full of doom. 'That was the Blair Witch donkey.'

They all started to giggle. Amber poked him in the ribs. 'Don't start us off again.'

Alex handed Paulo the drilling tool. It was like a giant corkscrew, with a handle and a long twisted shaft. 'Bore two holes in each tree, opposite each other and one slightly below the other. The one below creates a weak spot; the one above pushes the trunk over.'

Paulo nodded. 'Like a topcut and undercut when you're felling a tree with a saw or an axe?'

'Exactly. And make the undercut so that the tree falls outside, not in towards the landing zone.'

Hex picked up the machete. 'I'll clear some of the smaller bushes.'

Alex took the wrapper off one of the sticks of plastic explosive, then tossed it to Amber.

Amber caught it on reflex, then realized with horror what she'd got in her hands. 'What did you do that for?'

Alex laughed. 'PE's virtually inert. You could put it on a fire and it would barely burn.'

'Very funny,' snapped Amber. Her heart was still hammering. 'I bet you weren't so cool about it when they did the same to you on your course.'

Alex smiled sheepishly. She was dead right. He'd been shaking like a leaf when the instructor had tossed the stick of PE at him. You couldn't pull the wool over Amber's eyes.

Amber sniffed the PE. It smelled of nothing and felt like plasticine. Strange stuff. 'How is this harmless substance going to blow down a tree?'

Alex touched the small box in the kit. 'These detonators. You don't want to play catch with those.'

'Do you want this back?'

'Pick up the box. You can help me put it in the trees.'

Alex went to the first tree. Paulo had made two nice big holes. Now the question was how much PE to use. On the course – with the Territorial Army back at home – he had learned that even a small piece could blow a hole in steel. But trees? A lot of these had just withstood a minor earthquake and probably many others in the past. They'd be pretty tough. His instructor had given them a tip: when in doubt, add P for plenty. He had then proceeded to demolish an entire house instead of merely putting a hole in the front wall so maybe he'd gone a bit too far. Alex looked at the sticks in Amber's hand, picked one up, and squashed it into the hole. He took another one round the other side and did the same.

'Hey, you're really going for it,' said Amber.

'Trees are heavy,' replied Alex, moving on to the next marked tree. 'They take quite a bit to shift.'

'So long as you don't shift all of us as well.'

They continued until all the trees Hex had marked were drilled and plugged with PE. They'd used nearly all the sticks.

Paulo put the hand drill down next to Alex's bergen. 'So what's next?'

Alex took a small box out of the metal case and picked up a reel of cord like white washing line. 'This is det cord. I need one helper—'

Everyone said, 'Me,' but Li got there slightly ahead of the others. Alex handed her the reel of det cord and the knife he kept at his belt.

'Everyone else get into the middle of the landing zone with the injured guy,' he said. 'Then you'll be as far away from the blast as possible.'

While Paulo, Amber and Hex started moving the robber on the stretcher and all their gear, Alex and Li went over to a tree. Alex opened the box and revealed the detonators: silver tubes about the length of a pen top, with two wires coming out of the end. He picked one up as though he was lifting a mouse by its tail and pushed it into the explosive. 'You have to be careful with these. The heat from your hands can set them off so you have to handle them by the wires.' He did the same on the other side of the tree, using a slightly different detonator. The upper charge had to go off fractionally before the other to push the tree over, and so he used a slightly slower detonator. 'OK, I need some of that wire.'

Li paid out the white cord from the spool. 'How much?'

Alex took the end. 'I need two pieces about thirty centimetres long.'

Li slit two lengths of cord and handed them to him. 'How will you set it off? Light it?'

Alex carefully twisted the wires of each detonator onto the det cord. 'No. They're electrical. There's a firing device in the kit.' He knotted together the two ends and tied in a third piece so the arrangement hung like a necktie around the tree. 'Right, we need to feed out the wire and connect it to the firing device.'

Li paid out the cord until they were back to where the others were waiting with the bergens, chainsaws and the injured robber.

'Alex looks rather pleased with himself,' said Paulo. Sitting on his bergen he looked like a holidaymaker waiting for his flight to be announced.

Alex put the remaining detonators carefully on the ground and cut the det cord. He picked up the last mysterious item from the kit – a small black box with a hand grip. Two wires trailed from it. He twisted them onto the white cord at his feet. When he finished his eyes were glittering. 'This is the firing device. We're ready. Cover your ears.'

Hex nudged the robber and tried to show him he should put his hands over his ears. The man glared at him; his usual expression whenever they brought him water or checked he was OK. Hex pointed to the others – they nodded back at him encouragingly, their ears protected, all looking like the monkey who would hear no evil. The man seemed to realize what was going on and did the same.

Alex squeezed the handle on the firing device.

There was a small flash. The sound of the explosion was like being banged on the head. It echoed through the jungle, sending birds and animals scattering.

As the ringing in their ears cleared there was a sound of splintering. In moments the tree was on the ground, a pale ragged disc of freshly exposed wood facing towards them. It had landed exactly where it was supposed to.

Alex punched his fist in the air. 'Yes!' Amber put her fingers between her teeth and let out a piercing whistle that scared away any lingering birds. Paulo and Li gave each other high-fives. Hex sat and grinned. The robber let out a string of angry-sounding words.

'Go on,' said Paulo. 'Do the next one.'

'Go for it,' grinned Amber.

Alex and Li set up the next one and joined the

others crouching in the middle. This time, when Hex mimed to the robber to cover his ears, he scowled and put his hands up immediately.

There was a furious bang, and another tree capsized away into the jungle. The group's cheers and wolf whistles were almost as loud.

'Could you do a couple at a time?' said Hex.

Alex nodded. 'Don't see why not.'

When he and Li came back to take cover again, there were two trees connected by a garland of det cord.

Bang. They fell into the undergrowth. Five grinning faces looked around at each other. Even the robber was catching the spirit of triumph and smiling.

Hex looked up. For the first time in a few days, he was seeing sky. 'Hey, it's getting lighter.'

Paulo pushed his sleeves up and felt the sun on his bare arms. 'The sun at last. Hurry up and take down some more trees, Alex.'

Amber sighed. 'Ah, sunlight. Any longer in that tree canopy and I'd have seasonal affective disorder.'

'What's that?' said Paulo.

'It's that thing called SAD – you know, it's when

people get depressed in the winter because they don't get enough sunlight,' said Hex.

Li and Alex came back. Everyone covered their ears. Another bang. Now they didn't seem so loud. Hex and Amber carried on where they had left off.

Amber grinned like a snake. 'I know how they treat that. You have to sit in front of a glowing box for hours every day. Just like Hex does.'

Paulo chuckled.

'Who would have guessed you were going to say that?' rejoined Hex.

'For our next trick,' called Li, as though she was talking to a circus audience, 'we will do three at once.' She gave a quick bow and was met with cheers and whistles.

Alex and Li retreated to their safe positions to detonate.

Three trees were swiftly dispatched.

The next trees were the big mahogany that Amber had spotted, plus several oaks. Li and Alex ran back to take cover. 'These are big ones,' panted Alex. 'Might be a bit louder than before.' He sounded very pleased about it.

'The boy is definitely having too much fun,' said Amber.

They put their hands over their ears.

The bang was certainly bigger. It left their ears ringing. The oaks fell immediately but the mahogany remained upright. There was a great sound of groaning wood. Alex patiently waited for it to fall. The tree had been standing for hundreds of years. Of course it was likely to resist. A hunter had to expect that sometimes its prey would put up a struggle.

Then he went cold all over. It was finally starting to tilt – towards them.

He jumped to his feet. 'Run!'

9 CHAINSAW HELL

The tree's huge shadow loomed over them as its canopy blocked out the sun. Paulo and Hex grabbed the stretcher. The others were already running for their lives.

The tree's topmost branches rasped against another tree on its way down. A moment later they were lashing against Hex's back as he ran with the foot of the stretcher. He put on a spurt as it touched him, nearly pushing Paulo over at the front. There was an almighty crash behind him as the tree hit the ground.

Cautiously, Amber, Hex, Paulo, Alex and Li looked up. The tree was right across the landing zone, a big hulk of wood like a beached whale.

Five faces looked at Alex. For once, even the robber was silent.

'Just to let you know,' said Paulo patiently, 'the touchdown surface should be free of loose materials such as leaves and twigs. It should have no holes, tree stumps or rocks.'

'I don't suppose a blob of PE is going to fix that,' said Amber.

Alex stood up, staring at the mess in disbelief. 'I must have miscalculated the weight of the tree.' He ran his hand roughly through his blond hair.

'Or got the detonators the wrong way round,' said Li.

Alex cursed himself. How could he have made a mistake like that? He'd done all the others correctly.

'Where are our bergens?' said Amber.

Paulo swore. 'And the chainsaws?' He scrambled to his feet.

Hex's voice came out as a strangled scream. 'The night vision goggles!' He rushed forward after Paulo, lashing out with his arms at the branches in his way. Behind him, the others followed, cursing.

Hex's bergen was nestling between two heavy branches, unscathed. One of the chainsaws was next to it, along with the fuel cans and an orange chain-mail suit.

Alex found his bergen. The main trunk had missed it by centimetres. Paulo was dragging his away from the tree, pulling at it angrily as the straps snagged on branches. Alex didn't often see the laid-back Argentinian looking so annoyed. But if Paulo's bergen was OK that meant they'd still got the medical kit. Maybe everything would be unharmed. Thank goodness they were all unhurt. Alex yanked his bergen out, taking it back to where they'd left the stretcher – their new 'camp'. How had he made that mistake? Maybe he should have added P for plenty.

Behind him he heard Amber saying, 'Oh lovely. That's just swell.'

Alex reached the stretcher and looked back. Amber was surveying her bergen, her hands on her hips. She glared at Alex. 'It's squashed.'

'So's mine,' said Li. 'Flat as a pancake.'

'One of the chainsaws is under there too,' said Amber. She gave a tight smile. 'But that doesn't matter because the other chain-mail suit is there as well.'

Hex propped his bergen up next to the stretcher. He saw the robber looking at it rapaciously and realized he knew it had the mask in it. 'Oh no you don't,' said Hex, and moved it well out of his reach. Then he had a vision of the priceless mask with a big dent in it. Just to be sure, he checked. It was fine: it was well protected.

'So, Alex,' said Li, 'what happens now?'

Alex winced. He took a breath as though he was about to say something, and winced again.

Amber, staring at him from the wreckage of the tree, spotted his hesitation. 'Spit it out, Alex. What else could possibly have gone wrong?'

'We'll have to spend the night here. The heli won't stop if it can't land and it certainly won't come after dark.'

'But it's not going to be dark for another three hours,' said Amber. She could feel her wait-a-while scratches flaring up again in protest. And the bite wasn't feeling too good either.

'It's going to take a lot longer than that,' said Paulo. 'On the ranch we couldn't shift a tree like this in three hours.'

Alex tried to make himself think positively. 'We've got enough rations to go round for tonight and I'm sure we can double up on hammocks. Or you can have mine.'

'Lovely,' said Li frostily. 'Who are you going to share with?'

'I'll sleep on the ground,' said Alex.

Paulo began to feel sorry for him. He looked more and more miserable by the minute. 'Don't be silly. You can't sleep on the ground in the jungle. Something will eat you.' He heard Amber mutter something but thought he'd better ignore it.

'All my dry kit's in that bergen,' said Li.

'Mine too,' said Amber.

'You can have my dry kit,' said Paulo. 'I don't mind.'

'Yeah, you can have mine too,' said Alex. He patted his waistband absent-mindedly. It was second nature to check he still had his knife.

It wasn't there.

He looked at the hulk of fallen tree. Was his knife under there?

Li watched him as he crashed through the branches, panic written all over his face. 'Alex?' she called. 'Here it is.'

Alex turned round and saw his precious knife. He crunched back to her. Her face was saying, All my stuff's gone but at least you've got your knife. He was going to be apologizing for this catastrophe for quite some time.

Hex went first with the chainsaw. The protective clothing was zip-on orange over-trousers and a top – two layers of fabric with chain mail sandwiched in the middle. They felt heavy, the kind of garments you'd wear in cold weather. As soon as he fastened them he felt his sweat glands gush into overdrive. He put on the goggles and gauntlets and pulled the starting cable on the saw. First time it didn't start. Second time it did, with a roar like a motorbike, and settled to a steady chugging. He pulled the trigger that activated the cutters and the chain with its vicious teeth became a blur. He put it against the spindly topmost branches of the tree and the blade sank through.

Alex took the collapsible water containers and went to fill them. Li, Amber and Paulo rigged a shelter over the stretcher with a poncho from one of the surviving bergens. The sun was beating down viciously on the area they'd cleared and although the robber's dark skin could probably stand it, he'd get dehydrated quickly.

As Paulo unfolded the poncho the robber berated him – as usual. But Paulo reckoned this time he did have a point. 'Don't blame me,' he said. 'Blame the blond guy.'

Li hacked wood into stakes with the machete and passed them to Amber. 'Anyone any idea what language he's speaking?'

Amber drove the stakes into the ground. 'Nothing I've ever come across.' She was the linguist of the group. 'But the ancient languages are still used in remote areas. Even Mayan – which was used by the people who built the tomb.'

Alex came back and set down two water containers

the size of large beach balls, then picked up another two.

Paulo grinned at him. 'Our patient's just put an ancient Maya curse on you.'

Once Hex had cut up part of the tree, they started to clear wood. They used the remaining two ponchos, sweeping the smaller pieces of wood onto them and carrying them like a stretcher. They took load after load.

After a couple of hours Hex was exhausted. His arms ached. Whenever he pulled the saw away after severing a branch his shoulders quivered as though he'd received an electric shock. His mouth was dry with the taste of wood; sweat dripped down the inside of his chain-mail protection and sawdust stuck to him like feathers on tar.

The others were flagging too. They'd got to thicker branches, and the wood didn't fit on the ponchos so easily. Amber and Alex tried to load one piece but it was such an awkward shape they couldn't manoeuvre it. Amber threw down the poncho, hooked the branch over her shoulder and tried to drag it away. It was unbelievably heavy. Alex got under the other end and together they staggered away with it. Who would have thought wood could weigh so much?

Li and Paulo weren't faring much better. Li's hands were slippery with sweat and raw from the rough bark of the tree.

Finally Hex turned off the chainsaw and threw off the goggles. His arms and ears felt like the saw was still going. 'Anyone else want a go?'

Amber stopped where she was, breathing hard. 'What is that noise? Oh I know. It's silence.' She swallowed to take away the dryness in her mouth. 'Is doing that more fun than doing this?'

Hex peeled open the zips of the chain-mail jumper and trousers and let them fall off him while he stood. He savoured the sensation of cool air on his sweaty camouflage gear. 'Yes, terrific,' he said. 'I'm loving every minute.'

'Actually, guys,' said Paulo, 'we've got about forty-five minutes before sundown. We'd better get our camp sorted.'

Alex looked down at the tree. The topmost branches had gone but they barely seemed to have made an impression on the massive trunk and sturdy lower branches.

Amber peered into the tangle of wood. 'No sign of my stuff, I suppose?'

'I didn't see it,' said Hex.

'Rats.'

'I think our lost luggage is staying lost,' said Li. 'We'll have to file a complaint.' She glugged back her entire water bottle in one go.

'Alex, can't you just wrap a piece of that plastic explosive around the trunk and give it a good blast?' Paulo suggested.

Alex shook his head. 'It's not like felling the tree where you can tell which way it'll go. God knows what would happen.' He expected another ratty remark in return, but they all looked too tired to muster the energy.

Hex picked up the chain mail and spread it out on some branches. He wouldn't be surprised if it had rusted by morning.

They dug into the three bergens for stoves, rations, hammocks and dry kit, and began to prepare the camp.

* * *

Night in the open came a little later than it came in the tree canopy. Without the covering of leaves they saw the sun set in an orange glow, the shadows of trees all around. Once the sun had gone down, the sky was filled with stars.

Amber and Li lay head to foot in one of the hammocks. Li wore Paulo's dry kit and Amber wore Alex's.

Li peered out from under the poncho. 'Hey, look at those stars.'

Amber, at her feet, looked out the other side. 'At last. The great outdoors.' She felt a fierce stabbing pain in her leg. 'Ow,' she shrieked. 'Li, did you bite me?'

'No, I did not bite you,' retorted Li from the other end of the hammock.

'Is there an insect on me?'

'No,' said Li. 'You've put on so much repellent and antiseptic you're asphyxiating me.'

Paulo checked on the injured man for the last time and climbed into a hammock with Alex, moving so that he was lying head to foot like the girls. 'Alex, move over, you're taking up the whole thing.'

'Sorry,' said Alex. He was shivering in his wet kit. When Paulo got in his body warmth was like a radiator.

'Hex,' called Paulo, 'how did you manage to get a hammock to yourself?'

'I'll swap with you at half time,' called Hex sleepily. He hoped they wouldn't bother. 'Anyway, I've got a partner,' he said. 'I've got the mask.'

'You can swap with me, mask or not,' growled Li. 'Amber's driving me mad with her scratching.'

But within seconds they were all asleep.

10 MR UNPOPULAR

The next morning the light woke them, just as the dawn chorus began like a shrill alarm clock. The first thing Alex saw was the big tree. It looked like there were acres of it. And they had ten hours to clear it all before the helicopter came or they'd be stuck there for another night. He tipped out of the hammock, cold to the bone, his clothes still soaking wet. Paulo got up and hobbled like an old crone to check the patient. The robber was still asleep, snoring happily. He seemed to be having the most comfortable time of all of them in his hammock-stretcher.

Amber took the first shift with the chainsaw. Now they were working on thicker wood she discovered it was a hideous job. If you didn't keep it cutting straight it would glance off a log and dive into the mud, blunting the blades. Either that or it would land on your chain-mailed leg and gnaw it like a piranha. It spat sawdust and sharp chips of wood the whole time. It vibrated until your eyeballs rattled. Wearing the protective gear was like being swaddled in chains.

This trip just got better and better. Amber had missed the sun while they were under the tree canopy, but now the heat beat down mercilessly, wringing even more sweat from her pores. The chain-mail clothes were like torture, but at least she was covered. The others were shrivelling before her eyes. They were tanned but it was completely inadequate for this level of sun exposure.

Alex stopped what he was doing and smeared mud on his face, the back of his neck and his arms. Hex, Paulo and Li followed suit. Without sunscreen, that was the best they could do. But it wasn't ideal.

On and on it went. There seemed no end to it. They rotated duties after an hour. Amber surrendered the chainsaw and Li took over. Then Amber had to fetch water for everyone, filling their water bottles, taking empty containers down a steep slope to a stream, bringing them back full and dropping sterilizing tablets in. If they didn't drink continuously they would get disorientated, make dangerous mistakes – not a good idea with a chainsaw. Fetching water was heavy work but it was blissful after the chainsaw. Then it was Li's turn for water duty and Amber moved on to shifting debris.

They broke for cold rations at midday. By then they had been shifting wood for nearly six hours.

Paulo gave out more rations packs. They were running low. Sweat had washed away most of his muddy attempt at sunscreen. 'We've got three,' he said. 'One between two.'

Paulo ate half his share and gave the rest to the robber. Alex shared with Li. Hex went to share with Amber. He saw her mouth had an unhealthy grey tinge – she was getting low on blood sugar. He made her eat first, then insisted she finished the entire thing. She hated accepting help but knew he was right, and they couldn't afford to have her go into a coma. She gave him a pack of glucose tablets from her insulin kit.

By early afternoon they had reached the main sections of the trunk. They were super fit, but the relentless heat, the constant heavy lifting, were taking their toll. Now Hex had the chainsaw again. It was harder to keep it steady; Amber, Li, Paulo and Alex were finding it more difficult to drag the logs away too. Sawdust clung to the sweat on their faces, coated their clothes, inched down their throats with every breath. But they had to be finished by the time the heli flew over.

Hex cut another piece of wood. It was the first of the slices through the thickest part of the trunk. Alex rolled it away like a giant wheel. It wobbled and fell over. Alex looked at it, fed up. For a moment he couldn't face picking it up. Li came to help. She got her fingers under it and heaved it upright again. Alex caught the other side. Together they wheeled it away like a giant hoop.

It caught on a hummock and capsized again. Alex tried to catch it. His fingers scrabbled on the splintery sides. It crashed to the ground, pulling him down.

Alex stayed still for a moment on his hands and knees. His right hand was exquisitely painful. A few metres away, the chainsaw droned on.

'Are you OK?' said Li.

'Yes,' gasped Alex. His face was white.

'No you're not,' said Li. She went round to his side and heaved the great disc of wood off his hand.

As soon as the pressure was released, Alex pulled away, grasping his hand. It throbbed so hard it felt as if it was exploding.

'Medic,' yelled Li above the wail of the chainsaw. 'We've got a man down.'

Paulo came over. Alex stood up and offered him the hand. He expected it to be huge and red, like in a cartoon. But it looked squashed and boneless, like a pack of sausages.

'Can you move the fingers?'

Alex tried to move them. The pain flashed as though he'd burned them.

Paulo looked at the hand. The index and second fingers were pointing gruesomely upwards as though they had been put on back to front. Possibly broken, possibly just dislocated. Normally he'd talk a bit to a patient, but the chainsaw was wailing in the background and he felt too knackered to shout over it. He took hold of Alex's right arm at the elbow, grabbed his fingers and pulled hard. The crack drowned out even the chainsaw. Alex's yell matched it in volume. Paulo let go.

Alex snatched the hand towards his chest and bent over it, protecting it from further assault.

'Sorry,' said Paulo. 'But now they're straight I can splint them.'

He used Alex's knife to cut a splint from the debris of wood and bound it with strips of Alex's dry T-shirt. Then he cut a sling.

'I can't wear that,' said Alex. It seemed like a final badge of uselessness. The bandage and the splint he could hide under his sleeve while he got on with things, but not a great big sling.

'You should,' said Paulo.

'But I won't be able to do anything. It'll get in the way.'

Paulo tied the sling on. 'You won't be able to do anything anyway. You can't pick anything up with those fingers.'

Alex grabbed the water container in his left hand. 'I'll do water duty, then,' he said angrily. He stumped off towards the stream. This was all he needed. They had only three or four hours before the helicopter was due. Now it would be down to the others to clear all the wood. He wouldn't be surprised if he was very, very unpopular by now.

Even fetching the water was a challenge. When he struggled back up the hill with the full container he could only use his left arm and the muscles felt like they were on fire. He dunked a couple of Puritabs in and looked for the row of empty water bottles lined up beside the bergens. But he realized he couldn't fill them – it took two hands to lift the container and tilt it.

Amber came up to deposit her other bottle, also empty. 'So what is this? Self service?'

Alex nodded. ''Fraid so.'

She didn't look amused.

Paulo came up to refill his water. 'Alex, you could take over looking after the patient.'

'Yeah, sure,' said Alex. He was glad there was something he could do.

Alex noticed that as they got more tired, they had more bumps and scrapes. When they came for water they had more and more rips in their clothes, bleeding knuckles, grazed arms. Li cut away a section and the lost bergens came to light, like archaeological remains. The metal frames were squashed and twisted.

Amber, clearing wood, picked them up and tossed them to Alex. 'See if there's anything in there that isn't as flat as a pancake.'

Alex opened a bergen and caught a strong whiff of camping gas. The stoves had been crushed and the gas cylinders had burst. He remembered how they'd considered using explosives on the tree remains. He'd been very tempted. Thank goodness he hadn't – he'd have blown them sky high. He carried the bergens off to dump them.

Paulo and Amber came towards him, wheeling another circle of tree between them. Paulo saw the bergens. 'Alex, are there any rations in there? I'm starving.'

Amber's face lit up. 'Rations!'

'Contaminated,' said Alex. 'I wouldn't touch them if I were you. I'm just getting them out of the way.'

They looked so disappointed that for a moment Alex thought they might run him down and snatch them.

Finally, the area was clear. A pile of wood remained in the middle for the fire, laid out in the shape of a giant letter H, for signalling to the heli as it went over. Alex went round touching a flaming torch to it. The others sat at the edge on the three packed bergens, exhausted.

'What if one bit of it goes out?' said Li. 'Then it won't say H, it'll look like a chair.'

'Or a swastika,' said Hex. 'Hope the pilot won't get the wrong idea about us.'

When the H was fully ablaze, Alex came back and joined them.

'*Hombre*,' said Paulo, 'I have to hand it to you. You don't mess up very often, but when you do, you do it in style.'

'I'm sorry, guys,' said Alex. 'Really sorry.'

The heli sounded different without the canopy. The first they heard was drumming in the air, then a high-pitched whine that increased imperceptibly, as though it had always been there. Then they saw it, a black torpedo in the sky with a circular blur of rotor blades like a halo. It circled away and came back.

Alex looked up. The pilot was waving.

Alex understood. He jumped up. 'He's seen us. Let's put the fire out, then he can come back.'

The heli circled away.

They seized the water still purifying in the containers. Alex started sloshing it on the fire. They'd spent so long fetching and carrying it and trying to conserve it that pouring it on the ground felt ridiculously naughty. He looked round and realized there were four containers aiming towards him, caps off. He only had time to yell as Li, Amber, Hex and Paulo gave him a good soaking. His energy levels soared like a sugar rush and he retaliated. Soon the five friends were all haring around the H as it sizzled and died, joyfully dousing it and each other with water.

Still laughing, they kicked the ashy debris out of the way so the heli could land.

11 BELIZE CITY

Airborne at last, the five friends strapped themselves in and relaxed. As the heli pulled away over the vast expanse of green, Amber put on the noise cancel headphones and used the satellite phone to call her uncle.

'Hi, Uncle . . . Yeah, yeah, we're all right. Sorry I couldn't send a postcard. Had a great time though.' A pause. 'Oh you know, we were just trekking and stuff. Now listen, we've got this mask. Great big gold thing; bit like Tutankhamen but Mayan – you know what I mean? Looks quite valuable.' Another pause. 'Oh no, how we got it was quite boring really. A local gave it to us for saving his life. Anyway, we wondered if you know anywhere safe to drop it off because it's probably a national treasure.' Another pause. 'Oh. Right. Can you call someone?' Another pause. 'OK, great. Bye.'

She ended the call and took the headphones off. Immediately she was deafened by the noise of the heli – the high-pitched whine and heavy rhythm of the rotors. Li and Alex were looking out of the window at the jungle receding below. Paulo was checking on the patient. Hex was also wearing noise cancel headphones and checking his e-mail on his palmtop. He was completely absorbed, the blue glow of the screen the whole extent of his world. Amber reached over and pulled one of the headphone cups aside.

Hex's world was suddenly penetrated by the shrill engines and hammering rotors. It shocked him out of his pleasant reverie like a drill in his left ear. He looked around angrily and saw Amber's grinning face. He knew he should just laugh along with her but the noise was too loud and intrusive. Plus he was knackered; he needed his downtime with his palmtop. He snatched the headphone back and put it back on his ear. The beat of the rotors and the sound of the engine dwindled to a far-off rumble, as though he was going underwater. Blissful quiet again.

Paulo was checking Alex's splinted fingers, feeling them gently.

Amber looked out of the window. What an exhausting couple of days it had been. They'd planned a straightforward exercise and what had they got? Night terrors, mad monsters, tombs, treasures, tremors – and too many trees. These friends of hers could turn a quiet stroll into a roller-coaster. It would be sheer pleasure to chill out for a while.

In two hours they were approaching Belize City. It was still green, but there were roads, which was a big change, and buildings – greying wooden houses with roofs of rusty corrugated iron, white adobe colonial-style houses roofed with red clay tiles, washing lines with colourful clothes drying in the twilight – all surrounded by deep green foliage, as though the jungle was trying to invade the city. It started to look more industrial: a cluster of corrugated iron buildings stood next to a big ravine that ran across the land like a scar.

Amber leaned forward and looked down. The sides of the ravine bristled with trees and undergrowth. A bridge had been built over it, but a grey ribbon of tarmac headed straight down into it, its surface cracked as though it was very old. Obviously there'd been a quake, the road had been rebuilt and the old piece left in the hole.

High-rise banks and offices reflected the setting sun in their windows like a giant fire. They passed over the silvery blue ribbon of Haulover Creek, the branch of the Belize River that cut the city in two. Traffic was queuing to get over the bridge, the waiting cars sending blue clouds of smog into the air. People were driving home after work. It was strange to see such normal modern things going on when they had been living such a basic, simple life barely a hundred kilometres away.

The heli continued north, over houses and then a

stadium. Now the Caribbean Sea was visible, glittering in the twilight, and, on the shore, the concrete runways of the Municipal Airport.

The heli circled out over the sea and came back in to hover over a slab of tarmac with a letter H painted on it. Amber thought of their flaming H in the jungle. That seemed far better. Much as she had been itching to get out – literally – there was part of her that wanted to stay out in the wilds, just her and her friends.

They touched down. Paramedics ran towards the heli with a stretcher, crouching low to stay clear of the rotors. Next to the ambulance a police car and a black police heli were waiting.

The door was pulled open. Two paramedics in green overalls got in. They bent over the injured man and checked his pulse, respiration and other vital signs. One of them yelled to Paulo over the heli engines, 'What happened?'

'He was crushed by a large piece of stone.'

'Have you given him any drugs?'

'No. We splinted the leg but didn't try to put it in traction,' said Paulo.

The medic patted Paulo on the arm. 'You did a good job stabilizing him. We'll take him now.'

Li and Paulo helped them unload the robber. They laid their makeshift stretcher on top of the hospital trolley that was waiting. Their sharpened stakes and dirty, ragged bandages looked like something the Flintstones had made next to the clean steel. The medics ran it away across the concrete runway to the waiting ambulance.

Alpha Force climbed out of the heli, heaved their bergens out and followed. Behind them the heli engine wound down and the rotors slowed, became visible.

The robber was loaded into the ambulance and a policeman got in behind. A doctor in white coat and green scrubs saw Alex with his splinted fingers. He looked at Paulo. 'More of your handiwork?'

'Afraid so,' said Paulo.

The doctor put a hand around Alex's shoulders and guided him to the open tailgate. 'Sit down and let's have a look.'

One of the paramedics came up to Amber, Hex and Li. 'Anyone else need a doctor? Any injuries, cuts, abrasions?'

'Yeah.' Amber rolled up her trouser leg. The scratches from the wait-a-while plant showed as red weals on her dark skin. 'These are driving me mad. I'm a diabetic, by the way.'

The medic squatted down and examined them. 'Leave your trouser leg rolled up and let the sun get to them. Now you're out of the jungle they should clear up by themselves. The bite as well.' He looked around at the others. 'Anyone else? All been taking your anti-malarials? All feeling well? No food poisoning?'

The doctor finished rebandaging Alex's hand. The ragged sling and boy-scout splints were in a rubbish bag and he now wore a proper splint and white bandage. 'I don't need an X-ray, then?' said Alex.

'No point. It's swollen like a ham and nothing will show up. It's all straight so if there's a break it will heal fine – just keep it splinted.' Alex remembered the crooked mess his hand had been after the accident and silently thanked Paulo for his finger-bending torture.

The doctor dropped a pack of pills into his hand.

'Use these painkillers. Now I think you'd better go – they're waiting for you.'

Alex hefted up his bergen with his good arm and stepped out of the ambulance. The black police heli was starting up and his friends were getting in it. Out of habit, he checked their expressions. No distress signals, good. Apart from the pilot there was another guy getting in with them, a man in a suit with dark Timberland boots. Funny combination. Someone who wasn't completely comfortable in formal clothing? He didn't look dangerous, though. Alex smiled to himself as he ran over. Call me paranoid, he thought, but I just can't easily accept lifts from strangers.

Amber and Li grabbed his bergen and put it with the others on the floor. Paulo and Hex hauled him in.

'This is Felipe,' said Amber, as Alex buckled himself in.

'Hi,' said Alex. 'Are we going to the police?' The heli wound up to full power and lifted off.

'No,' said Felipe. 'The museum. We didn't want to waste any time.' The heli drew away from the airport and swung away towards the city.

'Is this something to do with your uncle?' shouted Hex to Amber.

'Suppose so,' she yelled.

'He works fast,' said Li.

Below, rush-hour crowds queued in a fug of smog to get over the bridges from one side of the city to the other. It didn't look any different from when they'd come over fifteen minutes before.

'It's always gridlocked at this time,' shouted Felipe. 'We thought it was better to bypass all that.' He pointed at his ears. 'I'll explain more when it's quieter.'

The flight lasted only minutes. In no time they were coming down again, landing on a flat lawn in front of a long low modern building about the size of a football pitch. Beside it was a sign carved in stone: NATIONAL MUSEUM OF BELIZE.

'I would have thought it would be in Spanish,' said Li.

Felipe unbuckled his belt. 'No. English is the official language of Belize. Most of our street names are English.' He opened the door. 'Come in.'

He led them in through a marble entrance. In the

lobby stood a startling monolith, twice the height of a man. A female face peered out from two-thirds of the way up. The features were fine and oriental. Around the face was an elaborate construction of Mayan hieroglyphs and symbols.

'Wow,' said Li, 'that is so beautiful.'

'It's a stele from Lubaantun in the south,' said Felipe. 'We've excavated there but we haven't had the funds to restore it so it's just a jungle. We brought the best treasures here to save them. There are two more behind you but they're not as spectacular.'

As one, they turned round. Two more giant figures flanked the door. But there was no time to linger. Felipe was already hurrying through a vast hall to the right. This room contained a long, painted frieze.

Amber recognized the style: cross-legged figures in tall headdresses surrounded by more of the bubble-like hieroglyph symbols. 'We saw something like this in the tomb in the jungle.'

'Very probably,' said Felipe. 'There are undiscovered sites all over central America, but the jungle makes exploring difficult. It's often special forces who find them, on exercise.'

If Felipe had looked round he would have seen that his five guests were trying to hide enormous smiles.

'And when we do get there,' he continued, 'we find many of them have been plundered anyway.'

He led the way past glass cabinets. Alpha Force caught glimpses of old axes; needles made from slivers of bone; pottery decorated with the bubble hieroglyphs in fine brushwork.

To the left was a swing door marked PRIVATE. Felipe pushed against it with his back and ushered them into an office. After the vastness of the museum it seemed small and homely. A desk overflowed with papers; a kettle stood on a side shelf next to a couple of mugs and a small reproduction of the stele in the lobby. Around the room were photos of Felipe – mostly next to overgrown tombs like the one they'd just left. Only one photo showed him wearing a suit – a formal picture of him shaking hands with some mayor. Alex decided the rugged boots were Felipe's more normal attire – so why was he wearing a suit today?

'Take a seat,' said Felipe. 'Let's see what you've

got. John Middleton said it was gold.' He sounded a little sceptical.

Hex opened the top of his bergen and pulled out the object wrapped in his T-shirt. He unfolded the material, removed the top layer of cotton wool and laid it carefully on the desk.

Felipe gasped. For a moment he just sat there, looking at the golden object on the black material, the white cotton wool poking through on the under-side. Then he reached for it with both hands, lifting it on the T-shirt, as if he didn't want to touch the object itself.

'Hey, it looks rather cool, doesn't it?' said Paulo. He'd forgotten how impressive it was.

'Is it all right?' said Amber to Felipe.

Felipe seemed to come to from a dream. 'Have you any idea how rare this is?' He slowly turned it over, letting the black material fall away as he inspected the back of the mask. He picked up an eye glass to examine it more closely.

'How do you know my uncle?' said Amber.

'John Middleton? He's had connections with the museum for a few years.'

'Like what?' said Amber. She knew he had a lot of powerful friends but it wasn't often that she came across one in the flesh.

'Oh I don't know. It was in the days before they gave me this desk job.'

A phone rang. Felipe pushed papers around the desk and uncovered the receiver. He lifted it. 'Yes?' He still wore the black-rimmed eyeglass. With his heavy black Hispanic brows it made him look deranged. 'They're here already. Good. We'll be right out.' He opened his eye wide and dropped the eyeglass onto the papers. 'Are you guys ready to go on TV?'

12 CELEBRITIES

Felipe led them into a further gallery. They were expecting to see the TV crew – but what took them completely by surprise was the looming skeleton of a dinosaur. The huge gallery was home to a tyrannosaurus rex. The bones were dark brown, the skull, ribcage and forelimbs looming above them like struts in the nave of a cathedral. The bones of the spine snaked down and away to the back of the room like a rollercoaster track. In the distance, behind the dinosaur, the wall had been painted with a prehistoric jungle scene, punctuated by plaster sculptures of smaller dinosaurs.

'Come on, they need you over there.' A woman with cropped red hair and a museum official badge on her jacket was trying to move them on. Felipe was already a little further down the gallery, watching a man with a shoulder-mounted camera film a glamorously groomed woman in front of a three-metre-high stone carving.

Alpha Force went closer. They weren't the only audience. A small group of schoolchildren and teachers were watching her as she talked into a microphone and looked earnestly into the camera.

'I'm here in the capital at the National Museum, to hear how five backpackers made the archaeological find of the century.'

The five friends looked at each other. The find of the century?

Alex muttered, 'No wonder Felipe had to put a suit on.'

Li looked at their ripped, stained clothes. 'Damn, should we have dressed up?'

The glamorous woman finished her piece and the cameraman gave her a thumbs up. She turned to Felipe, who had been adjusting his tie over and over again. He only stopped because she grabbed his hand and shook it briskly. 'Felipe, nice to meet you. I'm Carmela Hernandez, Channel Five News, Great Belize TV. Are these the heroes?'

Carmela didn't wait for a reply. She had already decided how to stage-manage the situation. She took Amber by the shoulders, put her decisively in front, and set Paulo and Li on either side. 'If you two get as close behind the others as possible,' she said to Alex and Hex. 'No sneaking out of the side of the picture.'

Alex and Hex exchanged a look. They were trapped. No ambush could have been more professional. Sneaking out of the side was exactly what they'd had in mind. Alex felt himself blushing to his roots and Hex looked down at his boots; they were caked in jungle mud.

Carmela positioned herself beside Paulo. 'Right, stay where you are and I'll just ask you a few questions.' She nodded at the cameraman. 'Ready to roll?'

The cameraman gave her a thumbs up. Carmela thrust her microphone towards Amber. 'So tell me how you found the mask.'

Amber responded with natural confidence. 'We were camping in the jungle, about a hundred kilometres away from here. We came across this overgrown tomb.'

Carmela took back the microphone. 'And you had to fight off a tomb robber to get it, didn't you?' She thrust the microphone at Paulo this time.

Paulo wondered how she knew that, but he answered smoothly, 'Not exactly. We went in because we heard someone in trouble. A man had got trapped. While we were helping him I saw this mask looking at me.'

'And we've got the mask right here, haven't we?'

Li felt something tap her on the hand. Felipe was on his hands and knees, holding out the mask. Li took it, brought it up and smiled at the camera as though she had been holding it all the time. The cameraman panned to her just as Felipe scooted out of the way on all fours.

There was an audible gasp of 'Ooh' from the schoolchildren, followed by shushings.

Carmela, ever the pro, smiled into the camera. 'Well, you can probably hear what a stir it's caused here; and I can tell you that it's an awesome sight.

Felipe Gomez is the curator here – I'd like to bring him in now.' She turned away from Paulo to where Felipe had been positioned ready for her. 'Felipe, we can all see it's a beautiful work; would you like to tell us why the mask is so historically important?'

'Well, from the style I can tell you it was made between AD 250 and AD 900. There's only ever been one golden Maya mask found before in the whole of central America; they're usually jade. In fact Maya funerary masks are not that common at all. So that makes it a very significant find indeed. I'm very excited.'

Carmela took back the mike. 'You can't have done any tests on it yet, so what makes you think it's that old?'

Felipe grinned. 'Good question. You see this piece of silver in the mouth? It's associated with Chac, the rain god, and was an amulet of survival. There was also one in the mask found at Palenque in Mexico, which dates from AD 695 and is one of the finest treasures of that period.'

Carmela could see that Felipe was warming up for a full-scale lecture and wrested the interview back to Alpha Force. 'And it looks like you picked up a heroic injury to get it.'

Alex saw the black lens of the camera home in on his damaged fingers in the sling. He wanted to curl up inside. 'Yeah, we took a few knocks,' he said nonchalantly. Off camera, Hex's wry expression said, You great fat liar.

Carmela turned back to the camera. 'So there we are. We'll be talking some more to these real-life Indiana Joneses tomorrow, when they've had a chance to catch their breath. But for now, back to the studio.'

She lowered her microphone and looked at the others. 'We'll be back at about ten tomorrow morning. Is that all right?'

'Fine by me,' said Felipe, loosening his tie. 'Is that OK with you?'

'Yeah, great,' said Li and Paulo.

Hex and Alex grimaced at each other. Amber looked dubious.

The camera- and soundmen started to pack up their equipment, while the red-headed museum official faced a barrage of questions from the school teachers and their excited charges.

'How did she know about the tomb robber?' said Alex.

'I don't know,' said Amber sharply. She was trying to work that out too. 'I didn't say anything about that to my uncle.' She looked at Felipe.

Felipe had been loosening his tie; now he decided to take it off altogether. 'The journalists saw all the helicopter stuff and followed the ambulance to the hospital. Plus the police cars gave them a few clues.'

'Great,' groaned Amber. 'I didn't really want my uncle to find out about all that. He'll flip.'

'Everyone seems to move fast here,' said Paulo. 'You only called him about an hour and a half ago.'

'That was my doing,' said Felipe. 'I wanted to get it out in the open as soon as possible. You know that other mask I talked about? The other gold one?'

Amber nodded as Li handed the mask back to him.

Felipe took something out of his other pocket. It looked like a black handkerchief but as he shook it out they realized it was Hex's T-shirt. 'It was me who found it. I took it to the museum in Guatemala, where I was working. A government official was visiting when I brought it in. Everyone was very excited, especially when he asked to see it. He said he'd pay to have it tested so that we could see where it was made and when. The director of the museum couldn't refuse – he had to let him take it away.' Felipe wrapped up the mask as he talked. Cotton wool came out of more pockets and was carefully inserted as padding. 'We never got the mask back. A week later, he sent back something else, a really bad fake. It was nothing like the mask – didn't even look like it, wasn't even gold. The real thing was worth millions – solid gold and incredibly rare. And this minister just took it from under our noses. There was nothing we could do, because we hadn't gone public. No one knew what the real thing looked like. So today when John Middleton called me, I thought, That's not going to happen again. Now the whole country's seen it. The cameras did a good close-up. No one will be able to walk off with it in a hurry.'

'Hey, we've still got an audience,' said Paulo. The school party was standing watching them with interest.

Felipe grinned. 'Why don't we give a few more

people a close-up?' He took the wrapped mask over to the little group. There was a buzz of excitement as they crowded around him.

If Carmela was a pro with the camera, Felipe was a natural with the kids. 'For over a thousand years,' he said solemnly, 'this mask has been buried in a tomb, on the face of a great Maya lord.' He flipped back the black material. The party gasped in wonder as they saw the ancient mask up close. 'And these people over here are the brave people who discovered it,' he went on, indicating Alpha Force. 'They found the tomb being robbed and brought the robber back to face justice too.'

Several small faces looked at Alpha Force in wonder. Hex turned round to escape their gaze, but he could still feel them looking at his sweaty back. 'Tomorrow could be really embarrassing,' he hissed to the others.

'Oh I don't know,' whispered Paulo. He winked at a couple of pretty girls who'd decided he was more interesting than the mask. 'I don't mind being treated as a hero once in a while. Real-life Indiana Joneses. Dashing, brave—'

'Just so long as my uncle doesn't see the show,' muttered Amber.

'Can't we just go back to the jungle?' said Alex. 'Tell them we've got to look for the Ark of the Covenant?'

At that moment, the bones of the great tyrannosaur skeleton began to shake. Felipe stopped mid-sentence and looked up in alarm. The whole room was hushed. The bones of the giant shuddered and the wires that supported them blurred as though something had plucked them. The great skull nodded; the clawed front legs twitched.

Then, the next instant, it was still again.

Felipe relaxed. 'That happens all the time. You get used to it. That's why it's held up with tensioned steel cables.'

The three teachers looked unhappy. 'Is this the room we're sleeping in?' said one. She was plump and wore a chunky pendant set in Mexican silver.

'Take your pick,' said Felipe. 'You can sleep in here, the room next door, or—'

'I think it would be safer to sleep in the next room,' said the teacher. She glanced at her colleagues.

'Don't you?' The other two teachers – a well-built man in blue cords and fierce spectacles, and a petite woman wearing a simple gold chain – agreed.

The children seemed to have other ideas and made noises of protest.

Felipe hit on a way to keep the peace. 'Next door is where we keep the needles and axes. And they were all found in tombs anyway.'

The children brightened up. The teachers looked a little less happy.

'Or you might like to sleep in the jade gallery,' he suggested, 'which has a rather fine mural of the blood-letting ceremony.'

'I think we'll make do with the needles and axes,' said the man.

Felipe turned to Alpha Force. 'By the way, where are you guys staying tonight?'

The five friends looked at each other. Everything had moved so fast, they hadn't had time to think about it.

Alex tried one last bid for freedom. 'I don't suppose the heli would take us back to the jungle . . .'

'You know,' said Amber, 'my bite feels much better

now. I think I second that.' It was preferable to the complications of being grilled by a journalist eager for a swashbuckling story.

'They're coming quite early tomorrow,' said Felipe. 'I'll find you a hotel.'

'Actually . . .' said Hex. He tailed off. They all looked at him. 'Does anyone fancy sleeping with the dinosaur?'

The resounding chorus of 'Yes' nearly deafened him.

Felipe looked pleased. 'The more the merrier – I'm bringing my kids in later to join the school sleepover – they love it here. We've got extra sleeping stuff in the stores, so help yourselves. In the meantime, if you're hungry, the cafeteria is open for dinner.'

To the five Indiana Joneses, that sounded like an even better idea.

Hex was the first to emerge from Felipe's storeroom. His view almost obscured by the sleeping bag, roll and pillow, he headed purposefully for the dinosaur.

Amber watched him. 'No way will any teacher tell him he's not to sleep with the T. rex.'

'Quite right too,' said Alex, and manoeuvred past her after Hex.

'What is it with you boys and dinosaurs?' asked Amber.

Felipe stuck his head in. He'd obviously been home to collect his children because he had changed into jeans and a checked shirt. 'Have you got everything you need?'

Amber, Li and Paulo were sorting out three more sets of sleeping stuff. The cupboard was crammed with kit. Felipe was even better equipped than they were.

'Why have you got all this?' said Li.

'It's expedition gear,' said Felipe. He picked up a sleeping bag and handed it to Paulo. 'Don't worry, it's been washed.'

'I don't mind,' said Paulo. He picked up his gear and made his way out of the storeroom. Felipe shook his head and knelt down to look for something in a cupboard.

'Felipe,' said Amber. 'What's the press saying about us and this tomb robber? What kind of questions are they going to ask us tomorrow?'

'I don't know,' said Felipe. 'Does it matter?'

'Well, they've already got the wrong end of the stick,' said Amber. 'Carmela said we had to fight the robber off, but we didn't have any fights with anybody.'

Felipe grinned. 'But they probably think it makes a great story. Relax. Enjoy it. You'll look great on TV.'

Amber rolled her eyes to the ceiling. Li put a hand on her arm. Her expression said, Chill – it'll be all right.

'Where's the mask?' asked Li.

Felipe was still rummaging. 'I put it in the high security vault downstairs.'

Li and Amber might have been unimpressed by the dinosaur, but a high security vault was another thing entirely. Li stopped in the middle of folding a sleeping bag and stared at Felipe's back. 'Wow. What else have you got down there?'

'Lots,' said Felipe, his voice slightly muffled. 'Things that have just arrived and we haven't yet worked out how to display. More examples of the things we've already got on display – there's loads more pottery, which is fascinating to me, but if we showed it all people would get bored. Things we're sending to other museums. Tell you what, when we get out the mask for the programme tomorrow I'll take you down there.'

Now it was Amber's turn to be excited. 'You're on!'

Amber dumped her sleeping gear beside Li's. The others were standing by the mural of the prehistoric jungle scene.

Alex pointed at it. 'Spot the deliberate mistake.'

They all peered carefully. Li came up behind them. 'I give up,' she said immediately. 'Is it something obvious like they're wearing wristwatches?'

Alex ignored her sarcasm and pointed to a couple of stumpy-looking dinosaurs, feeding on a ragged carcass. 'That one. It's a plant eater, not a carnivore.'

'Oh yes,' said Hex. 'It's a bagaceratops.'

Amber, shaking out her sleeping roll, had been trying to keep out of this male-bonding exchange of dinosaur trivia, but that name was too absurd to be ignored. 'What's that – a dinosaur you make into handbags?'

'No,' said Hex primly, 'it says it down there. Bagaceratops. Late Cretaceous.'

Amber shook her head again and went back to bed-making. After handing them out to the children, Felipe had also supplied them with glow sticks – plastic rods containing fluorescent chemicals. Amber activated them by breaking the capsule inside and laid them on the floor between the sleeping bags. The sticks would glow like torches for eight hours.

'Lights out in one minute,' called Felipe from the next room. 'Then you're on your own.'

'Glow sticks on, everyone,' called the voice of a teacher. 'If you need to get up in the night you can't put all the lights on. Hide them in your sleeping bags until you need them.'

'Can't we see the animatronic dinosaur?' pleaded a voice.

'I told you, Jorges,' said Felipe. 'It's still in the workshop.'

'But you said—'

'It'll be ready some time next week, Jorges, I promise.'

Amber grinned. 'Sounds like that must be one of Felipe's kids.'

Hex, Paulo and Alex were looking at each other with wide eyes. 'Animatronic dinosaur?' they said, as one.

Li poked Paulo. 'Maybe if we're still here in a week you can see it too.'

13 BUMP IN THE NIGHT

The lights were out. The children were settling down in the axe gallery. In the dinosaur room next door, Alpha Force sat on their sleeping bags, around the starfish of green light sticks.

'You know,' sighed Amber, 'I was really tired when we got here, but now I can't sleep. Anyone coming for a wander?'

Hex rummaged in his bergen and brought out the night vision goggles. 'Give these another spin.'

'I'll come,' said Li.

Amber put on the goggles and adjusted them to

fit her head. When she looked through them the glow sticks in the centre of the room disappeared completely.

Hex, looking up at her, pulled a face. 'I saw that,' said Amber.

'Just testing. You look like a biceratops.'

'Biceratops?' echoed Alex.

Hex grinned. 'Well, if triceratops means horrible three-horned face . . .'

The others laughed.

Amber snatched off the goggles. 'Come on, Li, let's leave these philistines to sleep while we go and look at fascinating old things.'

The girls picked their way through to the next gallery. Li carried a green light stick. It illuminated just a few metres in front of them. The first thing they saw was a statue of a reclining figure holding a bowl on its stomach, with its face turned towards them. As the eerie green light glanced off its headdress and eyes it looked quite real, its expression strangely forlorn.

'It's a chacmool,' said Li.

'What's that?' said Amber.

'I don't know, that's just what it says here.'

Amber carried the night vision goggles but didn't bother to put them on. There were cabinets around the walls. She wandered up to them idly. They contained pieces of jade, laid out in neat rows. In the half light they looked like blobs of black glass. Further along there were hoops and amulets and necklaces.

Li fell into step beside her. 'What's up?'

Amber shrugged. 'It's silly.'

'Your uncle?'

'Yep.'

'I think you're making a mountain out of a mole-hill, Amber. He must know the kind of things we've done—'

'But we've always been under cover before. We covered our tracks. Now we're going to be on national TV as ninja temple warriors.'

'He might not see the programme.'

'Of course he will.' Amber trailed her fingers idly along a row of cabinets. She looked in but hardly noticed what was in them. 'He's connected with the museum – they'll have told him to watch the news.

And everything else. And who wouldn't watch their relatives on TV? Especially him – he's always trying to find out what I really get up to.' She sighed. 'I just couldn't stand it if he pulled the plug on Alpha Force. Or if he even threatened to.'

Li didn't know what to say. She gazed into a cabinet, collecting her thoughts. Then she spotted something. 'Hey, Amber. Look at this.'

Amber came over.

'Look at that label.'

Under a pair of jade ear hoops and a ring was a plate that said: BY KIND PERMISSION OF MR T. AND MRS J. MIDDLETON.

Amber looked at it. For a moment she couldn't speak.

'Amber?' said Li gently. 'Are you all right?'

Amber shook herself. 'I suppose my parents must have found some stuff while on one of their missions. And donated it here.'

'Just like us,' said Li quietly. 'History repeating.'

Amber's thoughts were a whirl. No wonder her uncle was able to pull strings so quickly. He'd pulled those same ones before. He'd known exactly how to get helicopters here too. Had he done the same for her parents? What had they been doing while they were here? Apprehending tomb robbers was a bit lightweight for them – did John Middleton imagine his intrepid niece had been fighting bandits, drug barons and all the other potential dangers the area had to offer? He'd surely fear the worst. But most of all, seeing the label made her feel quite strange. Amber hadn't known her parents very well. Moments like this were like suddenly being given an undiscovered snapshot of their lives.

Li put her arm on Amber's shoulder. 'It's nice. It's what we wanted, wasn't it? To carry on their work. We'll keep doing that somehow.' She looked further along the cabinet. 'I wonder if there are any more?'

Amber could feel tears pricking her eyes. She felt wrung out like a rag. She didn't want to cry, so she put the night vision goggles on to hide her eyes. All the shadows disappeared. The room instantly spread out, became green. She could see into every corner. It was all in shades of pale greeny grey. All the stonework looked hazy, as though seen through netting. She turned. Her heart jumped into her mouth.

Beside the chacmool was a glowing figure, reclining in the same position. It had wild white curly hair and it held its hands in the shape of a bowl. It grinned and the inside of its mouth showed white like a furnace.

Amber's heart was hammering like an express train. She was about to shriek at it but it put a finger to its lips, materialized into Paulo, then pointed. Amber followed his finger. A couple of metres away from the chacmool was another glowing figure. This one had short tufts of hair – Hex. Paulo pointed again to the doorway. A floppy-fringed chacmool had arranged itself there. Alex.

Amber wanted to giggle but she stifled it. She took off the goggles. 'Hey, Li, you should try these in here. They're interesting.'

Li heard Amber's voice wobble and thought she was trying to stop herself crying. She put the goggles on hurriedly to allow her a quiet moment and looked away. Then she saw the three glowing chacmools and got the shock of her life. She let out a strangled gasp.

Beside her, Amber was laughing. She tried to keep it quiet to avoid disturbing the kids two rooms away, and it came out like a high-pitched wheeze.

The boys got up and ran back into the other room. Amber and Li gave chase. Li had a perfect view of their glowing backsides. 'You can run but you can't hide,' she muttered.

She rounded the corner and saw them crouching at the other end of the room near the feet of the dinosaur. They were trying to stay very still and quiet. It was funny how people behaved when they were trying to be invisible. To Li it was like broad daylight. Amber came out with her wheezy giggle and put her hand over her mouth – as if the giggle would give her away, not the fact that Li could see her as clear as day.

Li ran forwards, not even bothering to creep.

And hit something, hard. She hit it so hard, her head buzzed.

The others, crouching down, not only heard the impact, they felt it through the dinosaur's skeleton. They got up and blundered backwards. Paulo shone his light stick around. Li looked dazed. She was frozen in horror, looking at the shaking, rattling creature. Every bone it had was trembling.

Had they knocked over the dinosaur?

Li asked herself how she could have been so idiotic.

She'd run into it because it was virtually invisible next to the bright glow of warm flesh.

The shaking stopped. Slowly, they all breathed a sigh of relief.

Li slowly peeled the night goggles off and wiped her brow. 'Phew, that was close. It didn't show up next to you lot. I simply didn't see it.' She put her hand on it. It was solid, like a great big piece of furniture. Her shin throbbed; her arm and shoulder on the same side felt as if she'd been hit by a baseball bat. She must have run into it really hard. She giggled. 'I've kicked a lot of people over in my time, but never a dinosaur.'

'For a minute,' said Paulo, 'I had visions of us trying to put it all back together like one of those five-thousand-piece jigsaw puzzles.'

'And having to finish it by morning so that no one knew,' chuckled Amber.

'I don't think we'd be the museum's heroes any more,' said Alex. 'We'd—' He suddenly came to a stop.

The dinosaur was shaking again.

'I didn't touch it,' said Li.

There was a crash in the next room – a sound of shattering glass. Something began to patter onto the hard stone floor.

Alex was sure his feet were trembling. He shone his stick down at them. They were moving – and so was the floor.

There was a metallic groan above them as the steel cable holding the upper part of the dinosaur gave a huge shake.

Alex screamed at the top of his lungs. 'It's a quake! Take cover!'

There was a terrible noise, like an avalanche. It came from deep in the ground, a rumble of power and menace that vibrated through their bones. Things smashed in the gallery next door as though they had been literally shaken to pieces.

Amber tried to run but the ground was moving. It was like being on a treadmill out of control. The floor heaved up like an ocean wave and threw her aside.

Paulo stumbled as he tried to stay on his feet. The last thing he heard was a great snapping sound. One of the cables holding up the dinosaur had broken. And then he was running. He didn't know where.

The ground kept trying to stop him, heaving under his feet, roaring at him.

The dinosaur bones were coming down like skittles. Alex dodged but the heaving ground tried to throw him back into their path. He had never been so terrified. He just thought, Run, run, run.

Li didn't know whether the screaming was her or the children and teachers sleeping next door. She heard a noise like a whiplash. The rest of the steel cables supporting the dinosaur snapped and came singing towards her. As she ran she found she was climbing. She didn't ask herself what it had been or where it was. She just climbed.

Hex wanted to hide, but there was nowhere to go. He ran into a solid wall and it throbbed with vibrations. It was like being a tiny insect in the power of some monster. He looked round. Amazingly he was still holding the light stick. He wished he wasn't. The dinosaur skull was crashing towards him like a missile.

14 SILENCE

Eventually, the rumbling stopped. The sounds of breaking glass stopped. The ground became still and solid again.

Amber opened her eyes. It was dark.

It was silent.

Where was she? It was like waking up from a dream in a strange room and not knowing where you were.

She felt around her. She had no light.

Why was it so silent? Why could she not hear any human sounds at all?

Then she heard something: pebbles skittering like pouring sand.

She froze. An instinct told her she mustn't move. Why? In case she started it again. Started what again?

And then she remembered.

The earthquake.

Panic took hold of her like a creature inside her fighting to get out. She almost screamed out there and then, but fought to keep it in. Where was everyone? She'd been with her friends, hadn't she? Where were they?

Why was no one making any noise?

Get a grip, she told herself. Am I hurt? She wriggled her fingers. All there. Toes worked fine too. So nothing broken. She shifted position and felt the bruise on her hip bone. Probably where she was thrown to the ground. Yes, she remembered that. It hurt.

She sat up. Her head bumped against something solid.

So, she was under something. Something big.

She put her hands up cautiously, felt the extent of her prison. A stone slab of some sort. But it didn't feel like stone. It felt warmer, like plaster. Then the layout of the room began to come back to her like a flash of film. There was a frieze in the corner. It had probably come off the wall and she was under it.

She'd have to push it off. But should she? Everything might start moving again. Now everything was still and she was safe. She mustn't do anything that might make it unsafe again.

There were no sounds. Why were there no sounds?

She felt like her brain was in a loop. She had no sense of time – she could hardly remember anything from before the quake. She might have been here for ages: hours, days. Had she already woken up before and asked herself these questions?

And then she heard a scream. It sounded like a child.

Of course. There were children sleeping in the museum.

Suddenly the air was full of screams. It didn't sound like pain. It was a strange, keening sound of pure animal fear. What's happened? it seemed to say. Help!

People in trouble, thought Amber. The sound was like a reboot for her scrambled brain. At last I know what to do.

She got up on her hands and knees and felt around. Near the bottom of the slab was a hole. How big was it? She got down on her tummy, her legs squashed up under her by the wall. Actually, was that the wall? She couldn't take anything for granted now.

She got one shoulder and an arm through. A moment of panic. What if she got stuck? No, think. The frieze couldn't be very thick. There were people screaming, she had to get out. She remembered some piece of information – where it came from she didn't know. If you could get your shoulders through a hole, the rest of you would follow. Perhaps it was from cave diving, that was it. She got the other shoulder through and her head emerged.

She blinked. The air was dusty, thick as soup. On the floor was a slender light stick, which glowed like a fat sausage. She dug her elbows into the ground and pulled herself forwards.

She was out.

Amber got to her feet, picked up the light stick and moved it around like a torch. The air was so thick, she could hardly see in front of her. It was like being in moorland mist. But she could see the devastation just in the small area immediately around her: a flat stone floor had become like the jumbled rocks at the bottom of a cliff.

And she could hear. Screaming, crying.

'Hello?' she called through the doorway into the other room.

A figure was already standing up, staggering around, crying. Amber tried calling back but her voice was drowned out by all the screams. It seemed to be coming from the walls, the floor, everywhere. This room was also heaped with rubble. One of the walls had fallen down, right onto the area where the kids had been lying. Around the room, piles of debris were moving, as though people were trying to crawl out of the ground.

Amber ran towards the figure, her feet crunching on broken glass from the display cabinets. It was a young boy in pyjamas, eyes wide, black hair frosted with dust. He stared at her.

Amber took hold of him firmly. 'I'm Amber. Are you hurt?'

As she spoke she looked down. The boy had bare feet. How had he managed not to cut himself running around on all this broken glass? There was no blood in the footprints he'd left. He was panicking; trying to talk to her but looking around wildly as though his legs were still trying to run. The top and bottom halves of his body wanted to do different things: one half sought human contact, the other needed to keep running.

Amber seized him firmly. 'What is your name?'

'Gabriel.'

'Have you got any shoes? You'll cut yourself.'

Gabriel looked down and saw his feet. His face scrunched up as though he was about to cry. Amber realized he thought she was going to tell him off.

'You stay here. Show me where they are.'

Gabriel pointed.

The screaming was all around her, coming from behind heaps of masonry. There must be kids and teachers buried in there. They didn't seem to know she was there. Maybe they were crying out just so that they could hear other human noise.

Keep calm, Amber told herself. You can only do one thing at a time. Get this boy wearing shoes and then there are two of you to help people. Amber went to his sleeping bag and found a pair of trainers. 'Here, catch.' She tossed them to him and he put them on.

In the sleeping bag next to his, a girl was sitting up. Rubble was strewn across it but none of the pieces seemed very big. She saw Amber and her scream became a sob. 'Help me.'

Amber knelt down. 'Are you hurt?'

The girl shook her head.

Amber relaxed. The girl probably just needed comfort, so she hugged her. The girl sobbed a little more and then relaxed. Amber pulled away and wiggled her light stick. 'Have you got one of these?'

The girl nodded. She brought it out of her sleeping bag. It was orange. It illuminated her haunted face like a Halloween lantern.

Amber smiled. 'Good girl. What's your name?'

'Rosa.'

'Hi, Rosa. I'm Amber. Now put your shoes on and come and help.' Rosa stared at Amber. 'Go on,' she went on gently. The girl reached into her sleeping bag and brought out a pair of trainers.

Two survivors found already. Amber began to feel a little calmer, more able to cope. 'OK, Gabriel, Rosa.

How many people were here tonight? I saw three teachers – how many children are here?'

'Eleven,' said Gabriel.

'And they were all in here?'

Rosa nodded. 'Think so. There was someone screaming next to me.'

'We're going to go round and help people out. Everyone you come to, ask them if they're hurt. If they're not hurt, help them out. If they are or if you're not sure, call me and I will come and look at them. Understood?'

They nodded.

Amber noticed a light switch on the wall next to Felipe's office. She tried it. High up on the wall, a severed cable fizzed and threw sparks like fireworks, then died. Amber switched the light off again, then asked herself why she'd just done that.

'Hey, guys,' she called to the kids, 'look for glow sticks first. We need as much light as possible, and that's also where people are likely to be.'

Rosa and Gabriel started picking through debris from the collapsed wall.

A mobile phone was ringing. At first Amber didn't

hear it against the background of cries; she only gradually became aware of it. It seemed so normal, so everyday – as if she was in a café or travelling on a train, not stuck in the middle of a disaster. She listened. It wasn't answered. That might be their first casualty.

Where was it coming from? She'd better get to it before the kids, just in case . . . In case what? Her thoughts trailed off and she didn't finish the sentence in her head.

It was coming from her right. She put the light stick between her teeth and started pulling away lumps of masonry. They were heavy. She had to drag them off and then get out of the way as they crashed to the floor. She stopped after she'd removed a few and listened again. The phone had stopped. Amber pulled more lumps of concrete off. Now there was a hole in front of her. She had a bad feeling about this. She angled her head and carefully poked the light stick in.

There was a face. The mouth was open and clogged with dust. It fogged his glasses. It was the teacher. Amber leaned in further. She took the light stick from her mouth and shone it into the hole. The man's open eyes stared up behind the frosted glass. Even the irises were frosted with dust. A large block of masonry lay across his throat. It must have crushed his chest and windpipe. He was dead.

A glow by the man's left shoulder attracted Amber's attention. His phone. Amber reached in and pulled it out. Its display was blinking. Missed call. She sat up. It felt wrong to take the property of a dead man but this was an emergency. And he could hardly have any more use for it.

Amber dialled the number for the emergency services. At least she could now let them know there were people trapped in the museum. It was unlikely anyone would think to look here otherwise.

It was engaged. Amber tried again. After a couple of goes it connected. Amber sat up, ready to talk, but it was only a message: '*All lines to emergency services are busy, please try again later.*'

Amber cut the connection. A moment ago she thought she'd have help. Now she was fighting a major battle alone again. They must be chock-a-block everywhere else going to hospitals, hotels, stations. She tried to call up the contacts book on the phone. Maybe she could call someone else, one of his friends. Anyone, to let the outside world know there were people in the museum needing help. But the display faded and died. The battery was dead. Amber put the phone back where she'd found it.

She wondered what to do about the body. Should she mark the position, tell the kids not to look in there?

Then she heard Gabriel calling to her.

Amber went back to see what he wanted. He was kneeling over a girl, who was lying flat on the floor. She was conscious but her right arm was pinned down by a large block of stone.

'This is Beatriz,' said Gabriel.

'Does it hurt, Beatriz?' asked Amber.

Beatriz nodded.

Amber looked at the girl and realized she didn't know what to do. She had a vague idea that crush injuries weren't straightforward and that you shouldn't move anyone who'd been crushed. But what if the girl was bleeding under there? The light was so bad she couldn't see and she just wasn't used to dealing with casualties. Paulo was. That was who they needed.

For a while, Amber had been pushing certain

thoughts aside, getting on with practical things. But now her subconscious rebelled and made her face them. You need Paulo, it said – and by the way, where are your friends?

Are they under rubble like that man?

Are you the only one who's survived?

Rosa and Gabriel peered into a hole near her, breaking into her thoughts. They were doing a great job.

'No one in here,' chirped Gabriel.

'Well of course there isn't, silly, there's no room.'

'Hey, guys?' called Amber.

The kids looked at her.

'Keep chattering like that. Do it everywhere you go. Your friends who are still buried will find it very comforting to hear you.'

They moved on to the next pile and Amber's thoughts returned to the label in the jade room. Her parents had been here. They'd left behind a clue, to be found one day like a holy relic by the people carrying on their work. But now it seemed like an omen. Her parents weren't alive any more. Lives change. Humans are fragile. What had become now of the next generation, Alpha Force?

15 LONE RESCUER

Amber watched as Rosa helped another classmate out. He got to his feet and took cautious steps. Amber interpreted his body language and could almost read his thought processes. Was the ground safe to walk on, or would it shake them like dice in a tumbler? Even after he'd got his courage back the boy limped. He was hurt. His injury didn't look very bad but it might be better to let him rest.

Amber went to help him. 'Hi there. What's your name?'

'Pedro,' said the boy.

'Pedro, I've got a very important job for you. Can you hobble over here? Lean on me. Sit down here,' she instructed him. 'I want you to stay with Beatriz here. She's hurt her arm and she isn't able to move right now. Can you look after her until help arrives?'

Pedro sat down. 'OK,' he nodded. He stared at Amber. All the others had done that too. Must be the shock, she thought.

There were fewer screams in the room now. Those who were still trapped could hear others moving about normally. But Amber kept hearing the occasional cry from other galleries.

'Listen up,' she called. 'Pedro, Rosa, Gabriel – I need to go and see if there are people trapped in the other galleries. You stay here, carry on doing what you're doing. Promise me you won't move from this room. All right?'

They nodded.

Amber took two light sticks. She'd start with the entrance lobby, see whether they could get out. She heard another mobile phone start trilling, then another, but she couldn't tell where they were. They weren't answered.

She reached the wall and her light stick picked out an urn on a plinth. That was odd. Then she realized she'd gone completely the wrong way, towards the dinosaur gallery. Without any landmarks and with so much devastation she needed a compass to find her way about.

In the doorway she held the light sticks up, making sure when she set off again that she wasn't taking another wrong turn. They glinted off the polished surface of the urn. Amazing, she thought. It's survived all this. For a moment she couldn't take her eyes off it, this proof of the randomness of fate. What about the rest of the dinosaur room? she wondered. That's where her friends had been.

Amber held up the light sticks. The dust was still thick, like soup, and the glow couldn't reach very far. She could no longer hear any screams or mobiles. Just that trickling sound of running stones. She ventured forwards.

A plaster bone pointed out of the gloom like the front boom of a ship in a heavy fog. Next to it another bone had broken in half, its broken surface gleaming stark white. She ran the light sticks upwards. The whole dinosaur was smashed. Part of the roof had come in on it too. She seemed to remember there was an office beyond it, but it was completely blocked.

She listened. Just shifting debris; nothing human. All the sounds were coming from the room where she had been.

Then Amber saw a big huddled shape on the floor. It was about the shape and size of a torso. She looked away, her heart in her throat, her thoughts running at double speed. She would have to look again. If it was a body, she couldn't leave it there. What if the children found it?

She took a deep breath. She'd look again in a moment. In a moment.

OK. She'd look at it now.

She waved the light sticks over it. Her eyes were closed. She made herself open them.

It was a bergen. Its top was still tied shut.

She unfastened it and spotted explosives and the detonating kit. Alex's. His bergen must have a charmed life. That was the second time it had escaped being crushed when other bergens had perished.

Tears pricked her eyes. She wiped them away.

She continued towards the jade room. With every step she searched the floor with the light sticks. It seemed to take ages to cross the dinosaur gallery. She remembered it being about twenty metres across but now the room seemed to open out into hectares. She peered into the jade gallery. It was the same story. Rubble, debris. Smashed glass glinted like heaps of jewels. Presumably among them were baubles of jade.

It didn't sound like anyone was in here either. She could hear mobile phones trilling softly, but they were behind her, in the direction she'd come from. Amber saw a phone on the ground and picked it up. She tried the emergency services again. Still the recorded message.

She turned and picked her way back. It was like walking along a rocky cliff at night. On she went. When her light sticks caught the big urn again she knew she was nearly back in the axe room.

What was that? She flashed the light sticks on it again.

It was moving.

Something smashed in the jade room. It must be an

aftershock. There were screams from the other room. The urn was toppling towards her. She grabbed it and staggered under it – it was like catching a big clay ball. She felt the earth quieten under her feet again.

'Not much point in saving that,' said a voice behind her.

It had a slight Spanish accent. Amber whirled, her arms still tight around the urn. 'Paulo!' She put the vase down and hugged him hard. 'Are you OK?'

'Yeah,' he said.

She ran the light sticks over him. He was cut and battered, his combat fatigues smeared with white dust, but otherwise he was intact.

Paulo was staring at her, like the others had been. Is he in shock too? thought Amber.

'Hold still,' he said. 'You've got a big gash on your forehead.'

'Oh, so that's why people have been staring at me,' she said.

Paulo had a look at it. 'It's stopped bleeding. Ideally we should wash it but I think you'll live. Any concussion?'

'No, I don't think so.' She sighed and gave him

another hug. 'It is *so* good to see you. Where were you?'

'In the jade gallery.'

'But I was just in there.'

'Yeah, I know. I saw your sticks. I called you and you ignored me and started to phone someone. So I decided to give you a surprise.'

Normally she'd have given him a thump but she felt too drained – and too pleased to see him. She sighed. 'There are so many strange noises in here. Listen to those cries. You have to tune them out. It's awful. Was there anyone back there with you?'

'I don't think so. I didn't hear anyone. I heard the screams out here and thought this is where everyone must be. But it's so dark . . .' He didn't want to finish the sentence.

'The dinosaur room's a mess,' said Amber. 'We can't search in there without proper light.'

They were both trying to avoid saying the obvious; that that's where the others had been.

'We got out,' said Paulo. 'They probably got out too.'

Amber nodded. 'Right.'

The sounds of activity from the axe room were becoming more organized. 'Sounds like you've been busy,' said Paulo. 'Come on, let's go back there.'

When in doubt, focus on a task. It stopped you thinking of unpleasant possibilities. 'I've got casualties for you to look at,' said Amber. She hefted up Alex's bergen. It might be useful.

Alex had little recollection of the actual quake. He just ran. And when he could run no longer he threw himself on the ground and curled up in a ball. For a long time he lay there while the earth shuddered around him. Gradually it steadied and calmed.

Then he heard the screams next door. That's when he knew he wasn't alone, that this wasn't a crazy dream – although it felt like a fit of madness. He wanted to scream himself but he fought to hold it back. His survival instincts were kicking him like a persistent bully. Do something.

Orientate yourself. He looked at his watch. Find out what time it is, and you instantly feel more in charge of things. He couldn't see the face of his watch. There was no light. No light at all.

Was he blind? Maybe that's what was wrong. Maybe he'd been hit on the head.

But no, he was seeing vague shadows. That's when another piece of information came back to him, like a picture seen on a TV screen. There were very few windows in the museum. It had a few horizontal slits high up, like windows in a military bunker. It seemed to have been built to keep light out. Well, they probably had to protect the artefacts.

When he envisaged the high slitted windows he remembered where he'd been running to. It was like he was reloading the memories, piece by piece. Now he had the map of the place in his head. He remembered he'd been running to the doors at the entrance, trying to get out.

He felt behind him. Now he had his back to rubble. So where on earth was he?

He'd got up on his hands and knees – or rather on one hand and both knees. He cursed the arm in the sling. Carefully he felt in front of him.

His arm had met only thin air. The floor had just vanished.

16 THE PIT

Paulo squatted down beside the children. 'Hi,' he grinned. 'Beatriz, will you let me see this arm?'

A lone mobile was ringing. Another started again. All these phones, hidden in the wreckage, thought Amber. Did that mean there were people under there too? She had an idea. She got out the mobile she'd found. Li had had her mobile with her. Why not try calling it?

Rosa tapped her on the shoulder. 'There's someone out there,' she said quietly. 'Someone in the next gallery. I heard a voice.'

Someone needed help. Calling Li would have to wait. Amber jumped to her feet. 'How long ago?' They hadn't checked the entrance gallery yet.

'A few minutes.'

'Good girl. Wait here.' She went past Paulo, who was joking with Beatriz to keep her calm as he examined a gash on her arm where the block had cut her. 'Paulo, Rosa's heard a voice. I'm going to check it out.'

Amber stepped into the entrance gallery. After the axe room it was stygian black. She waited for her eyes to adjust. 'Hello?'

'Amber, is that you?'

The accent was unmistakable. English, a very odd variety. Not Am-ber but Amb-er. Geordie. 'Alex!' yelled Amber. 'Where are you?'

'Here.'

She looked around. It was pitch black everywhere. She might have been looking into a cave or she might have had a mask in front of her eyes. 'Where?'

Something was moving about in front of her too. It was more than just the rubble settling. It sounded deliberate.

'Hello?' called a voice. It was high and panicky. 'Hello?' A woman.

Amber tried to peer into the dark even though she knew seeing was impossible. 'Are you hurt?'

'No. But I can't get out. I can't see anything.'

'I'm Alex.'

'I'm Amber.'

'Alex who? Amber who?'

'We're the backpackers,' said Amber. Her voice echoed across the room.

'Where are the children?' called the woman.

'We're getting them to safety. Are you one of the teachers?'

'Yes. I'm Señora Marquez.'

'Amb-er?' called Alex. 'What time is it?'

'Why?' said Amber. 'Have you got to be some-where?' She hadn't even thought about the time. She looked at her watch, waving her light sticks over it. 'Ten-thirty.' And then her brain made sense of the dim images she'd been seeing in the room. 'Oh.'

'What?' said Alex. 'What's wrong?'

'The floor's given way. Felipe said there was a basement, didn't he?'

'I think so.'

'The floor's collapsed into it. This room's a great big pit.'

Alex shuddered. It was weird enough hearing Amber's voice coming from a tiny point of green light. Hearing her describing things he couldn't see, couldn't even imagine, was worse.

'Alex, are you hurt?'

'No. I can wait here for a while. It seems solid enough.'

'Señora Marquez?'

'I'm not going anywhere, honey.'

'I'll be back when I can.'

'Amb-er?' called Alex. 'Who else have you found?'

'Paulo.'

Alex picked up on the note in her voice. She hadn't said anything about the others. He wasn't going to ask. 'You take care,' he said.

'OK. Back soon.'

He saw her move back into the other room, the light sticks reflecting green off her shiny dark skin, melting into the black.

He had a moment's panic: he was in the dark

again. He told himself to calm down. It wasn't so bad now. Amber was just in the next room; so was Paulo. And Señora Marquez was out there in the dark, waiting with him. Just knowing they were there made everything a whole lot better. Up until then all he'd been able to hear were sounds of earth falling, the masonry slowly crumbling, like water dripping in a cave.

Now he knew there were people alive in the next room. People moving about, helping each other, getting each other out. Making jokes. Surely the worst was over.

A green and orange glow appeared at the corner of the room.

'Amber?'

'Yep, it's me. Señora Marquez, I'm going to throw down a light stick to you. Ready?'

Alex watched it tumble like a fluorescent candy bar. He saw hands scrabble towards it.

It steadied, lighting up a giant set of eyes and a sensuous mouth.

It was like their nightmares coming to life. A giant, still cold face lying there in the dark. Alex yelped.

Amber shrieked. Señora Marquez dropped the light stick and made a high sobbing sound.

A voice came from high up, on the balcony. 'It's OK, it's not a body. It's a stele. It's stone.'

Alex's pulse quickened. 'Li?'

'Li?' called Amber.

Now Li could see them. A white lithe-limbed figure in the doorway – that was Amber. Someone in the pit beside the fallen stele. Alex on the edge of the pit. 'Yeah. It's me. Alex, don't move or you'll be in deep do-do.'

'Li,' called Alex, 'have you got the night vision goggles?'

'Certainly have.'

'Can you see the entrance?'

'Yeah. It's right behind you. Blocked.'

She saw Alex's shoulders slump with disappointment.

'Li, do you need help?' called Amber. 'Are you hurt?'

'No, I'm fine. And I can probably see a lot better than you guys can so don't worry about rescuing me, I'll sort myself out. How are the others?'

'Paulo's in the axe room being Florence Nightingale. Haven't seen Hex yet.'

'He'll turn up,' said Li.

'Where are you?' called Alex. 'You sound like you're somewhere in the sky.'

'Remember the cafeteria? Up on the gallery?'

Alex consulted the map in his head. The cafeteria overlooked the entrance lobby. 'Oh, good move.'

'Yeah, I can't get down. But I'm working on it.'

When the quake hit Li decided to aim high. She was up the rough stone wall and over the parapet in a flash. She was aiming to get out of the skylight at the top but the walls started to crumble. All she could do was dive under a table, protect herself. The table started to inch across the floor, shaken by the vibrations like a pea on a drum. Li gripped the legs and went with it, like a turtle trying to keep an unruly shell on its back. Debris thundered down onto the table, minute after minute. Would she be buried, wake up in a tiny square coffin between toppled blocks of broken masonry?

Finally the shaking stopped. What now? She heard

the screams far off. It made her think of going to sleep in the jungle and hearing the animal calls. She had the night vision goggles. She pulled them over her head and switched on.

The floor of the cafeteria was littered with stones and dust. It looked as though someone had tipped a mountain of builder's rubble over the tables and chairs. Some of the pieces of masonry were more than a metre long. The table had saved her from a nasty injury.

Where was the skylight? She was sure she remembered a skylight. Oh no. The pile of rubble was a section of the roof. So no more skylight.

It was then that she registered that the goggles still worked. Well, when they got back to civilization she would thank the manufacturer from the bottom of her heart. She obviously felt a hell of a lot better than those poor people moaning in the dark.

She remembered there were stairs. She got out from under her shell and went to look. One wall of the cafeteria was glass bricks. It had collapsed into the staircase. At first it looked surreal, like the crystal gardens she had made in junior school.

Cautiously, she put a finger on a jagged edge. It was knife sharp. It would go straight through her jungle boots.

Then she'd heard the others. As she'd leaned over the balcony, talking to Alex and Amber, she thought about jumping. But it was too far, especially with the collapsed floor.

She remembered seeing a fire hose coiled up on the wall. If it was still there maybe she could use that to climb down. She went to look for it.

Paulo was using an ancient axe to dig out another child. He had a new helper, Consuela, a pretty seven-year-old who was pulling at a lump of concrete with fierce concentration.

Amber delivered her news. 'We've found Li. She's got the night vision goggles.'

Paulo's entire face flooded with relief, his handsome features ethereal in the ghostly green light. It was such a change that Amber realized he'd been fearing the worst. It confirmed her own fears – if someone wasn't found they really could be . . .

Paulo understood like a mind reader. 'Hex will be

out soon,' he said, as though it was simply a matter of time. He put his dusty hand out, patted her leg and left a big white print on her thigh.

Amber swiped at him playfully with her light sticks. 'Don't you wipe your hands on me, cowboy.' But his easy Latino confidence made her feel everything would be all right.

The kids were working hard. Axes chipped on stone and concrete. It was like being in a mine. Phones were still ringing, buried under the rubble.

Pedro and Beatriz were talking on their phones. Although Beatriz had been freed, she wasn't allowed to join in with the rescue – Paulo decided her wound was too deep and the thin scab of clotted blood might split if she moved too much. So she and Pedro kept each other company.

Pedro finished his call. Amber pounced on him. 'Did you get through to someone?'

'I got my dad. He's OK.'

'Did he say how bad it was anywhere else?'

'It's bad,' said Pedro. 'We live in Hutson Street and the house next door has gone.'

Amber got out the mobile she'd found. Did Hex

have his mobile? She might as well try. She dialled and—

Suddenly, as one, the ringing sounds stopped.

Beatriz took her phone away from her ear and shook it. 'It's gone dead. I was talking to my mum.'

The hands on the axes were stilled. 'Why have the phones stopped?' said Gabriel.

Everyone looked at each other. Just as they'd made another link with normal life, it had been cut.

Damn, thought Amber. I should have phoned Hex earlier.

Paulo spoke. His voice sounded ominous. 'The cells must have gone down.'

A skitter of debris started to fall, like wind picking up. Was it an aftershock? Was that why the cells had gone down?

Hex woke suddenly. He opened his eyes and immediately he was dazzled by a bar of bright green, like an alien craft landing. He put his hands up in front of his eyes and tried to push the thing away. It clattered and bounced.

A light stick.

OK, that wasn't so bad. He picked it up.

He tried to sit up and banged his head on something hard. Could this day get any better?

Then he remembered. That dinosaur head angling towards him, its wide mouth like a shark's. He'd rolled away and scrunched into a ball. Something must have hit him on the head. His mouth tasted of cement.

He was under something – what? He turned his head, carefully this time, holding out the light stick. It was hoops of stone, like archways. He was under the ribcage of the dinosaur – it was as if it had swallowed him. Around him was the fallen skeleton. Hex had a moment of panic. It was all around him, no way out.

Calm down, he told himself. The ribcage had protected him.

In his mind's eye he conjured up a picture of a tyrannosaur skeleton. He'd learned its parts like a religious mantra when he was four. Most of the tyrannosaur's mass was in its back end. The bones at the front were smaller and there were fewer of them. If he could work out which was the front end, there should be fewer bones – and that would be the end to start digging.

He looked up. The ribcage was wide where he was, narrowing rapidly behind him like an understairs cupboard. So that meant he should dig the other way.

He pushed against a bone. It fell with a clatter that echoed. That was good. Outside there was a big space. He pushed another. One by one, bone by bone, he dismantled his prison, slowly and methodically. Finally he emerged on his hands and knees.

Now he was out he could hear things moving. It sounded like steadily sliding rubble. Was that the sound of people talking? And mobile phones? He looked round. Behind him the fallen dinosaur had made an impenetrable barrier, like a wall. Next to it, a funerary stone had fallen off the wall. It was still intact and formed the other part of the enclosure. All the time, debris was falling like light rain.

In front of him was an office. Someone was in there. He held up the light stick and waggled it. 'Hello?'

A woman came out. She had short dark hair with

dust frosted on top like icing sugar and smeared across her face like war paint.

'Hi,' he said. 'I'm Hex.'

'Susana. I was trying on my mobile but it's gone down. Here, maybe you can make it work.'

Hex took the mobile. Having something so normal in his hands was a huge relief. He tried the screen. 'There's no signal. Maybe the cells have gone down.' He touched his belt pouch, where his palmtop was. He'd check the signal on that.

Suddenly Susana lurched towards him. The floor was shaking again. The pile of dinosaur bones was trembling. Hex got down and curled into a ball again. There was a great bang like an explosion and they were falling, the sound of thunder in their ears.

17 STARTING AGAIN

Paulo grabbed Consuela and Rosa and held them in a huddle on the ground. Amber did the same with Gabriel and Vicente, a boy they'd just rescued. Pedro and Beatriz clung to each other. Rubble bounced around them like bullets. Then a roar came that seemed to split the very fabric of the building. The children were screaming. It was worse than the most terrifying clap of thunder and it went on and on.

They could see nothing, didn't dare to open their eyes. The thunder died but the shaking carried on. Paulo briefly thought he should try to relax and go with the movement instead of tensing against it, as though he was falling off a horse, but all reason was driven out of his head. It was horrible. He just wanted it to stop.

Alex tried to cling onto something, but there was nothing. He felt himself falling. Li, up on the gallery, had a perfect view. The rubble began to push Alex into the pit like a bulldozer. Below, beside the stele, Señora Marquez was trying to run, but the ground kept moving under her feet like a treadmill.

But then Li had problems of her own. There was a groaning like ripping steel. Masonry sprayed her, stinging her arms and face. The next moment all was still again. A bare girder had appeared in front of her like a spear. The tremor had shaken it out of the concrete roof.

It fell towards her.

There was rubble behind her and no room for her to get out of its way. She grabbed it as it went past, curling her arms and legs around it like a monkey. It took her down towards the ground, its sharp front edge moving like a javelin. It was heading for a wall.

Should she jump off? Below was a pit of rubble – she'd probably hurt herself more landing in that than if she stayed on the girder. She bowed her head to protect it and caught the night vision goggles. She'd forgotten she was wearing them. What if they smashed, sending pieces of glass into her eyes?

Too late to take them off now. She buried her head as flat as possible and closed her eyes.

As Alex tumbled into the pit he saw the girder sliding past, Li riding it like a whale.

Then he hit something. It was hard and it was metal. The clang reverberated through his skull like a great kettle drum. He bounced and scrabbled to get a grip. Both hands grappled and found a pipe. His injured fingers sang with pain but he was slipping. He closed his eyes, gritted his teeth and pulled for all he was worth, putting most of his weight on his good left arm. When he felt the pipe under his chest, supporting him, he stopped to catch his breath.

Alex felt a massive impact as Li crashed into the front wall. He clung tight to his perch, concrete showering over him. Li tried to melt into the girder.

Rubble pounded her shoulders and back as the girder lanced through the wall like a sword.

It stopped, nearly flinging her off. The first thing she noticed was the cold air. She looked up: the point of the girder had embedded itself in the ground. She was outside, on the front lawn. And the night vision goggles were still functioning. They were certainly getting a workout tonight.

Someone was shining a torch at her. It dazzled her through the goggles and she switched them off. The figure came to help her down. She saw that it was a man with a spanner in his hand; his arm was soaking wet.

'Are you all right?' A woman stood behind him, looking at Li nervously.

Li rolled off the girder like an acrobat and landed on her feet. 'Yeah. Who are you?'

'We live just up the road. We got out of our house. We wanted to help. We just turned off the stopcock on this water main. It's flooded the road.'

It seemed the quake was over. The ground was still. But what a scene of devastation. Li put the goggles on again to see more detail. The roof of the museum had caved in on one side. The front wall was shattered where she had come through it on the girder. Further along there were big cracks. On the ground outside, the cracks carried on through the paving slabs, as though a vein had been drawn down the building and onto the ground. Water seeped from an open manhole cover where the man had turned the supply off.

'That was quite an entrance you made,' said the man. 'Or should I say exit. I'm Jose, by the way. And this is my wife Imelda.' Imelda nodded. She was carrying a sledgehammer.

'Li.'

'We were on our way down the road. I didn't think there would be anybody in there.'

'There are loads of us in there,' said Li. 'We need help.'

She walked up to the hole in the wall and slipped through.

Inside the building, she heard the cries again. That animal, panicked sound, like the aftermath of the first quake all over again. No one could trust the ground they walked on any more.

For a moment she felt like joining in but she forced her mind to focus. She grabbed the torch from Jose's hand and shone it into the pit. 'Alex, are you all right down there?'

'Yes. Fine.' His voice was hushed. She could hear he was shaken.

She put the night vision goggles up to her eyes for a moment. Alex wasn't much better off than before. He was stuck on a duct from the air conditioning equipment, still at least two metres off the ground. 'Stay where you are, Alex,' she called. 'Don't try to go anywhere. Señora Marquez, are you all right?'

The teacher was huddled in a ball among the broken masonry, protecting her head with her arms. She had a fresh coating of dust but aside from that seemed intact. 'I – I think so,' she said shakily. She glanced behind her into the gloom. 'I think I can hear something back there.'

'We'll send some people down,' said Li. 'Just hold tight. Don't go off in there by yourself.'

'Don't worry, honey, I'm not going anywhere,' came the tart reply.

Li took the goggles off again and turned to Jose

and Imelda. They were staring towards the screaming, their faces shocked. 'I think they need our help in there,' said Li. She was about to lead them to the axe room when something made her check first, something on the brink of her hearing. She stopped dead still for a moment, listening.

Then she heard a very familiar voice.

'Say "yes" when I call your name. Beatriz?'

'Yes,' called a voice.

It was Paulo. He was doing a roll-call of the children.

Li let out a huge sigh. For a moment, all the horror was forgotten.

Paulo went through a list of names and ended with: 'Amber?'

'Yeah, yeah,' said Amber in her characteristic drawl. 'Don't get drunk on power.'

Li strolled through to the other room. 'Hey, guys,' she said. 'I've got a torch, a sledgehammer, night vision goggles and some extra pairs of hands.'

Then she nearly dropped the lot as Paulo grabbed her in a bear hug.

Amber grinned at her. 'What took you so long?'

'I was just finding the way out.' She looked around at the room. It was well lit because of the light sticks, but the ceiling and stone artefacts had been reduced to piles of rubble. Broken glass and stone axes littered the floor. Several children sat wide-eyed, looking at the new arrivals, their pyjamas and hair covered in grime. 'This looks bad.'

'We'd just got it under control,' said Paulo. 'Now it's chaos again. We'd cleared a good amount of rubble and freed all those kids and now the quake has rearranged it all.'

'Come and bring those goggles in here, Li,' said Amber. She led the way to the dinosaur gallery while Paulo gathered the children to introduce them to Imelda and Jose. 'We haven't looked in there yet – there was no noise so we concentrated on looking where there was.'

Li followed Amber into the room and put the goggles on. It was very different from the last time she'd looked at it. She couldn't believe the devastation. The dinosaur had gone completely. Where it had stood, arching over the space, was a pile of rubble, like a wall after a demolition. The steel cables that had supported its head had left huge chunks where they'd pulled out of the wall. Half the wall to the jade gallery had gone too, leaving a ragged, round hole like a rough archway. Li walked forward cautiously and then stopped.

The floor rocked under her foot. It was like treading on the edge of a cliff.

Amber saw Li's foot wobble. Then Li performed an incredible move. First she put all her weight on her back foot, then she sprang backwards like a ninja. When she whipped off the goggles, she was breathing hard.

'Jeez, I saw that,' said Amber. 'It moved.'

'The floor's gone,' gasped Li. 'If anyone steps on it they'll go through. Don't let any of the kids come in here. I can't see anything that looks like a person. Here – you have a go.'

Amber raised the goggles to her eyes. She saw nothing but varying shades of stone.

Li was breathing a little more easily now. 'Señora Marquez says she thinks she can hear people down in the basement. I think that's where we need to look next.'

'Yeah,' said Amber. They went back into the axe room.

Paulo had pulled Jose and Imelda to one side to brief them. 'When you find someone, can one of you take over and check them out? We're trying not to let the children see anything upsetting.'

The two newcomers nodded.

'And keep them away from that corner,' he added quietly, looking towards the dead teacher. 'There's a body.' They nodded again and went to start work.

Li beckoned Paulo over. 'Right, guys, how many are still missing?'

'There were eleven children in the party,' said Amber, 'and we've found six.'

Paulo suddenly had a thought. 'No, there are more than eleven. Felipe said he was bringing his kids in.'

'Oh Lord,' said Li. 'Did he say how many?'

Imelda had overheard their conversation. 'Felipe Gomez, the curator? He's got two children – Ana and Jorges. I used to know his wife.'

'Thanks, Imelda,' said Paulo. He turned back to the two girls and continued in a low voice. 'There were three teachers too. I remember them from earlier. The man's dead, Señora Marquez is in the lobby, so there's still one to find.'

Li looked around. 'Where's Hex?'

Amber looked down resolutely at the goggles. 'We haven't seen him yet,' she said. Then she seemed to realize what she was looking at. 'If someone was lying dead in that room, would it have showed through these?'

Paulo and Li thought for a moment. Behind them the regular chink as axes pulled away concrete began again as Jose organized the children to look for survivors. It was Paulo who replied. 'I think so. It takes a few hours for a body to lose its heat. You'd definitely have seen if there was anyone there that we could get to.'

'I'll go and search the basement,' said Li.

She was the obvious choice. Her climbing skills were better than anyone else's and her tiny size meant she could squeeze into spaces that tall, willowy Amber couldn't get into.

Amber handed her the goggles. 'I'll stay here – Paulo, you go with Li in case someone needs medical help. If we have a medical emergency here I can holler for you.'

'And,' said Li, 'we'll get Alex out. It's time he did some work, broken fingers or not.'

'Hang on,' said Paulo. 'Just getting supplies.' He pulled a bergen away from the wall, brushed the dust off it and opened the top.

'Whose is that?' said Li, incredulous.

'Can't you guess?' said Amber.

'Yes, folks, it's Alex's amazing indestructible bergen,' said Paulo. He pulled out a water bottle, green nylon poncho and dry kit, then fastened the top again. 'And once we get Alex we'll have anti-septic too from his survival kit.'

'Ow,' said Amber. She bent and rolled up her trouser leg hurriedly. 'Get me some while you're at it.'

Paulo, kneeling on the floor, tried to get a look at her leg. 'I thought the wait-a-while infection had gone.'

'It has. But the bite hasn't. Every now and again it really hurts. As though I've caught it on something.'

Paulo went back to Alex's bergen. 'I can't see anything. It'll probably go down soon.' He laid the items he was taking on the poncho and tied it into a bundle, then stood up.

Li fixed the night vision goggles on. 'Let's go.' She followed his broad back out of the room.

Amber saw Jose and Imelda moving the kids away from a pile of rubble and beckoning her over. She knew what that meant. They'd found another survivor. Or a body.

18 TRAPPED

Hex had had a dream. He was falling. There was thunder, like boulders raining into a big steel bin. There was screaming, like seagulls rising in the air. He was in a cage with curved bars arching over him while a hurricane hurled bones at him like skittles. One of them hit the cage and it turned into spun sugar and shattered.

Maybe the dream had lasted only an instant. Suddenly his eyes were open, clogged with dust. He blinked hard. He breathed and then coughed.

There was a green glowing stick poking out of

the ground. A bewitching light in the murk. It was the only thing he could see. He grabbed it.

A voice gasped. A frightened, female sound, like a gulp and a scream.

'Hello?' said Hex. His voice took a couple of goes to work, like a car that hasn't been started for a while.

He pulled the light stick out of the ground. He blinked again and moved. He was in a small space. He tried to turn round, but his bruised bones banged against hard stone. Everywhere there was hard stone. Against his shoulders, his knees, his feet, his head.

Where was he? Panic began to rise in his throat. His hands felt around. He felt like he had been locked in a small box of hard stone and squashed down until they could put the lid on. Everywhere, his fingers met sharp pieces of stone. Strange shapes loomed out of the green darkness. He remembered the dinosaur.

A hand reached out and grabbed at him. He flinched and jumped.

A pair of eyes blinked back at him. They were above him, looking down.

'Susana?' The name just came to him. Of course. It was the girl from the office. Short hair, pretty face.

'Hello?'

'What happened?'

'I think it must have been another quake. Or an aftershock.'

'Shh. Can you hear that?'

They listened. There was the usual hiss of moving pulverized concrete, like a rain of sand. There was a bigger sound, of a lump of masonry smashing. And there was a moan, far off, like the cry of an animal in the night.

'Hello?' called Hex loudly.

There was no answer. There was no echo. It was a very small space.

'Are you OK?' said Susana. She looked like a rag doll that had been squashed into a shelf in a cave wall. Was that how he looked? Was he really in a space that small?

Hex felt like he had gone ten rounds with a heavyweight boxer. Every surface was bruised. He was acutely aware of every knobble on his frame: his elbows, his vertebrae. He shifted position and winced. But it all seemed to work. 'Bit bruised,' he said.

'Me too. My tummy hurts,' she said. 'Where are we?'

He tried to get a mental fix on where they were. There was nothing but dinosaur bones around him, as though he had been thrown into a pit along with them all. How heavy were they? He remembered the noise, the great rumble like a landslide. Had they gone through the floor? How many bones were there in a tyrannosaur? Probably enough to make it very heavy.

He felt like he couldn't breathe – his lungs had shrivelled to raisins. He needed air. He was stuck in a pit, buried by dinosaur bones.

Li stood on the edge of the pit, night vision goggles on, Alex's abseil harness over her shoulder like a handbag. She held onto the fire hose. Paulo tested it: the big red drum still seemed firmly attached to the wall. 'It's solid. Go.'

She jumped off the edge and wrapped her legs around the hose. Paulo paid the hose out from the wall while Li descended.

Alex was on a duct about halfway down the front

wall. Debris had piled up on it so it looked like a shelf for storing broken concrete. Señora Marquez was at the bottom, sitting next to the stele.

Li attended to Alex first. He heard the sound of something swishing close to him in the dark. She landed lightly, hardly making a sound. He'd have known her anywhere. The nozzle of the hose clanged against the metal duct, making him jump.

'What's that?'

'A fire hose.'

'Lovely. I feel like a cat being rescued from a tree.'

Li put her hand out and he stood up carefully – the first time he'd dared get upright. He didn't share Li's head for heights and anyway, he didn't have anything to hold onto – except her. Plus there was a pipe that ran down the middle – the one he'd clung to during the second quake. It was handy then but it might be easy to trip over now. 'How are we going to get up?'

'We're not going up. We're going down. Put this on.' She shipped something off her shoulder. He felt webbing in his hands: his abseil harness.

Alex threaded himself into it awkwardly, protecting

his damaged fingers. Li fastened it and threaded the end of the hose through. 'Will that hose take both of us?'

'I certainly hope so,' said Li. 'Ready?'

'Yes.'

Li cupped her hands around her mouth. 'Let us down, Paulo.'

Paulo paid out more of the hose. Alex started to descend, then Li hopped onto the rope above him. She looked down as they descended. Alex saw his own face as two tiny reflections in the night vision goggles.

Then they were down. Li hopped off the fire hose while he fumbled one-handed to get out of the abseil harness. It felt so good to feel his feet on solid ground again.

The two friends walked carefully over the uneven rubble to where the teacher was lying.

Alex put out his good hand for her to shake. 'Señora Marquez, we meet at last.'

The teacher held the light stick up to him. She said sternly: 'You're much younger than I thought.'

Alex grinned. 'So are you.' Li heard and gave him

a look. Through the night vision goggles it was a very severe look indeed. He didn't blame her. The remark was smarmy in the extreme. However, he'd sensed teacherly disapproval in Señora Marquez's voice. If he didn't disarm it, she might decide she didn't trust him to make decisions. Flattery seemed the best way.

Li remembered the goggles looked a bit scary and took them off. 'Señora Marquez, do you have any injuries?'

'No, I'm fine.'

Paulo called down from the lip of the chasm, 'Señora Marquez, how did you get down there? Was anyone with you?'

She shook her head and called up, 'I don't know. I didn't know where I was going. I just ran. How are the children? I keep hearing them up there.'

'We've got quite a lot of them out already,' said Paulo. 'Our friends are searching for more.'

Li offered her the abseil harness. 'We can get you up there. Then you can join them.'

'No, I'll stay and look for the other children with you,' she said. 'They're my class.'

Alex stood up and they helped Señora Marquez to her feet. 'Right. One light stick each, and we've got the night vision goggles.' He found he was grinning like a loon. It felt so good to be doing something again, rather than being a victim.

'Hang on,' said Paulo. 'I'm coming down.'

He'd barely got the words out when Amber's distinctive tones rang through to them from the axe room: 'Paulo! Quick!'

'Guess I'll see you guys in a bit,' said Paulo, and sprinted to help her.

Amber was on her hands and knees. She was halfway under a large slab of concrete, a piece of ceiling as big as a billiard table. One corner of it was supported by a granite plinth. 'Get in here,' called Amber. 'We need mouth to mouth.'

Paulo put down his pack, threw a light stick to her and in seconds was squirming past her to get under the slab. Although he was big, he was supple and quick. He saw a small body in pyjamas, lying on its back, mouth open.

The slab was so big, there was plenty of room

underneath for two. Amber slipped in beside him and felt for a pulse. 'Heart's beating but pulse is weak.'

Paulo wiped the dust from the boy's mouth and tilted his head back. Amber was shining the light stick so he could see. No obstructions in the mouth. Paulo held the nose with one hand to close the nostrils, put his mouth over the child's and exhaled.

Amber was watching the chest. It should have risen as Paulo blew into the lungs. 'Nothing's happening. And the pulse is weakening.'

Paulo straightened up. There must be an obstruction. His mind raced. He had to move the child, but he didn't know if there were any injuries. He remembered the ABC of emergency medicine: airway, bleeding and circulation. Get him breathing first. 'Support his neck,' he said to Amber.

Amber put her hands under the child's neck. Paulo rolled him onto his side, thumped hard between his shoulder blades and pulled him back. Then he tilted the head back again and blew gently into the lungs.

'They're inflating,' said Amber.

After a moment, Paulo slowed to see what happened.

The boy coughed, then moved normally, arching his body up. Paulo felt a huge wave of relief. No neck injury.

'He's breathing on his own,' said Amber. 'Shall we put him in the recovery position?'

Paulo rolled the child onto his side, then wriggled down until they were nose to nose. 'Hello,' he grinned. 'Are you hurt?'

The child's voice was faint. 'No.' He started to shiver.

That wasn't good. Paulo called towards the opening, where several young faces were watching. 'Can someone find a sleeping bag? We need to keep him warm. He's in shock.'

A voice came back: 'Can't see one.'

This really wasn't good. Shock was serious. If the boy's body temperature dropped too low he could die.

There was a small commotion outside and the heads in the opening jostled for position. 'Alejandro!' called a voice. 'Is he all right?' It was Vicente.

'Is he your friend?'

'Yes.'

'Are you really good friends? Good enough to hug him?'

Vicente's face went serious. He nodded.

Paulo beckoned him in. 'Come here. He needs your body heat. I want you to cuddle him like this.' He demonstrated, putting his arms around the child, his body close to Alejandro's chest. Alejandro's shivering eased.

Vicente squirmed into the hole and Paulo pushed him into position. Vicente looked a bit dubious.

'Have you heard of the Malvinas War, the Falklands?'

'Yeah,' said Vicente enthusiastically.

'Well, this is what the soldiers did to keep each other alive.'

'Really?' Vicente looked a bit happier.

Paulo and Amber moved out of the way and the little boy snuggled down next to his friend. As Paulo squirmed out he saw the big vase on the floor next to the doorway – the vase where he'd first found Amber. That's where that plinth had come from.

'When did you find this?' he asked.

'Just now,' said Amber. 'All this rubble fell away and we had to find something to prop it up with.' She touched his arm. 'Paulo.' He followed where she was looking. Further along, right at the end of the space under the slab, a woman was lying in the rubble. Only her head and torso were visible; her legs were obscured by another big piece of concrete.

Paulo squirmed along until he was next to her. Her eyes fluttered open.

'Hi,' he said. 'How are you?'

'OK, I think. Stuck.'

'Well, let's have a look,' said Paulo.

Amber watched from the entrance as Paulo flashed the torch into the hold. A ragged lump of masonry lay across her thighs. It made deep creases in her sleeping bag. To do that it must be very heavy.

A voice whispered in her ear. Gabriel. 'It's Señora Zapata.' His face was solemn.

Paulo was talking to the teacher. 'How long have you been trapped like this? Just since the second quake?' But he already knew the answer. The piece of wall must have fallen on her while she slept and she didn't stand a chance of getting clear.

'No. Since the first.'

Paulo whistled. 'And it's taken us all this time to find you.'

She sighed. 'I've been sleeping, waking a bit, sleeping some more. I couldn't exactly come out and help.'

Paulo needed to think. What should he do? The first quake was hours ago. He remembered the decision he'd had to make when they found the robber in the tomb. The robber had only been like that for a short time, minutes at most. This was different. After a few hours the damaged tissues would have built up a lot of toxins and when she was released . . .

Jose peered through the hole. 'Is it safe to start clearing?'

Paulo didn't want to tell her the truth of what a bad state she was in. He pretended to inspect the lump of concrete. 'No, I think we'll need a crane to lift that,' he said.

'I don't think so,' said Jose. 'If a few of us get under that end—'

Paulo didn't want to have a debate about it. The facts were nasty. He shimmied out of the space, got up and took Jose to one side. 'She will die as soon as we release her. We must not move her until there's an ambulance here.'

Jose looked at Paulo sceptically. He was at least thirty years older than Paulo – about the age of his father. He probably doesn't see why he should take orders from a mere teenager, Paulo thought.

'I think we should move it,' said Jose. 'She must be better off without that thing on her. I'll move it if you can't.'

Paulo bit his tongue. He realized Jose felt threatened by him and wanted to prove he was stronger. How could he convince him?

'Please,' he said quietly. 'That's how my uncle died. A piece of farm machinery fell on him and we moved it. The doctors said if we'd waited, they could have given him some drugs and saved him.' The story was a complete fabrication but Paulo was desperate. 'It was so horrible,' he added. 'I felt guilty for years.' Maybe if he looked vulnerable the silly man would feel superior enough.

Jose tried to push past him.

In the blink of an eye Jose was on the ground, his arm up behind his back. Amber was sitting on top of him. Paulo watched wide-eyed. She leaned over and muttered in his ear, 'Why don't you listen, you macho jerk? This is life and death, not a weightlifting competition.' She released him.

He got up slowly, his face mutinous. Amber stared back at him. Her face said, If you try that again, you know what I'll do.

'Suit yourself,' said Jose in a surly voice. 'But I think you're wrong.'

Amber put her arm through Paulo's. 'We'd better go and reassure Señora Zapata. She'll be wondering why we're not moving her.'

Paulo crawled back into the small space.

'Can't you boys get this off me?' said the teacher. 'You look big and strong.'

Paulo took a deep breath. 'Señora, I don't think we should move this until an ambulance is here.' He told a little white lie. 'Just in case there's some damage we can't see.'

Señora Zapata nodded slowly. Paulo didn't know how much she was reading between the lines.

A giggle came from Alejandro and Vicente.

'I'll stay here and keep an eye on these little monkeys, then,' she said.

Paulo patted her on the arm. 'If I'm not here and

someone tries to move this, tell them they can't unless they show you a blue flashing light.' He squirmed out.

Everyone seemed to have come to a natural break. The children were sitting quietly with Beatriz and Pedro, sharing out sweets from Amber's emergency supply. Jose and Imelda had flopped down against a heap of rubble. They looked exhausted. Amber dug into her insulin kit and offered them a pack of glucose tablets. 'Try these. They'll help you keep going.'

Imelda took the pack and peeled off a couple of the tablets. 'Thanks.' She looked up at Amber. 'It's easy to get upset when you're tired.'

Amber shrugged. 'No hard feelings?'

'No hard feelings,' said Jose.

Amber sat down with her back to the wall of the dinosaur gallery and closed her eyes. A half-peeled pack of glucose sweets dangled from her hand. She looked drained. Paulo settled down beside her. 'Amber, don't bite my head off but I have to ask – are you keeping up with your insulin?'

Normally Amber hated it when the others fussed

about her diabetes, but she knew he'd made an important point. In an emergency it was easy to think so much about others that you forgot to look after yourself. 'I'm fine. I don't need to take it until morning. I'm keeping track of time, don't worry.'

Paulo ran a hand through his hair. 'Well, you're doing better than me. I've lost track of time. I feel like we've been here for ever.'

Amber sighed. 'I'm not physically tired, more emotionally. They're getting harder to rescue and they've got injuries.'

Their voices had got quieter and quieter. Paulo whispered, 'Señora Zapata . . .'

Amber leaned forward and put her head in her hands. Then she looked at Paulo. 'Surely she must be in pain?'

'I don't think she is. I think shock is preventing her realizing how massive her injuries are.'

'She said she'd been sleeping.'

Paulo shook his head. 'I don't think she's been sleeping. More like having blackouts.'

'So she's being brave.'

'Or it's the shock talking. Hey, Amber.'

'What?'

Paulo leaned closer to her. 'Where did you learn to do what you did to Jose?'

Amber smiled, her eyes still closed. 'Li taught me a few of her moves.'

Paulo grinned. 'I thought it was in the Cheong style.'

A new sound echoed through the galleries. A sharp sound; a crack through the air.

Amber's eyes were wide open again. 'Those were gunshots.'

19 LOOTERS

Alex and Li heard the shots and acted on reflex. They each clapped an arm around Señora Marquez and hit the deck.

Alex saw a pile of concrete; debris shuttled into the corner by the tremors. That would do as cover. 'Over there,' he hissed. 'Keep low.'

Li kept her arm across Señora Marquez. She felt the woman hesitate. 'Move,' she said sharply, 'or we'll be shot.'

The woman didn't argue. They squirmed on their bellies, pulling themselves along the dusty floor with their elbows.

Another shot rang out. It ricocheted off a piece of concrete.

But the three were safely behind the pile of rubble.

Li sat up. 'Why would anyone be shooting at us?'

'I don't know.' Alex put on the night vision goggles and peered out cautiously. The dark basement hopped into clear visibility like a channel change. He scanned upwards. Two figures were up in the entrance hall, glowing like radioactive snowballs.

'Two shooters,' whispered Alex.

Another shot. Then a voice through a loudhailer. 'Come out with your hands up.'

'And then what?' hissed Li to Alex. 'They shoot us?'

Señora Marquez was silent. Her eyes were darting from Li to Alex, wide with fright.

Alex looked again. 'They look like police, so maybe they won't shoot.'

'Are you sure? They were shooting a moment ago.'

Alex checked. The shape of the holsters, the glint of light on the badge, the outline of the peaked caps. 'They're definitely police.' He took the goggles away from his face and looked at Li. 'We'll have to go out there. If they come down here and flush us out that will be a lot worse.'

Señora Marquez swallowed. 'Flush us out?' she asked hoarsely.

Alex nodded to Li. OK? She nodded back. Alex shouted to the policemen, 'We're coming out. Don't shoot.' He took a deep breath and stood up, his hands in front of him and visible.

Li did the same.

A powerful torch stabbed out of the darkness, making their eyes water. It was high up; about the level of the entrance hole Li's girder had made. It made the voice disembodied; they couldn't see beyond the torch. 'Come out into the open.'

They stepped forwards carefully onto the rubble. They could hardly see. Loose chunks of masonry wobbled under their feet.

'We have orders to shoot looters on sight. For the last time, throw down your weapons or we'll shoot.'

Looters? 'We're not looters,' said Alex. 'And we don't have any weapons.'

'You are holding a weapon in your hand.'

'They're night vision goggles.' Alex stopped, got

his balance and held them in the beam of light so they could be seen. 'Not a weapon. We're looking for survivors.'

'Why are you in the museum? It's closed. There's no one to find.'

'There's a party of schoolchildren. They were staying the night.'

Señora Marquez spoke for the first time. 'I'm their teacher. From the Baron Bliss Memorial School.'

'You're not all from the Baron Bliss School,' said the voice. 'They don't have any teachers who are English.' The voice sounded dehumanized though the loudhailer.

Li gave Alex a desperate look. How were they going to explain who they were?

Alex had an inspiration. 'We're the backpackers who were on TV this evening . . . yesterday, I mean. We found the mask. In a tomb in the jungle. We were on the news.' He looked at Li.

Silence. The light continued to shine from the corner of the sky like a pitiless, interrogating god. Li looked at Alex again. The police didn't believe them. 'Who was that woman who interviewed us?' hissed Alex.

Li racked her brains. It came to her. She spoke out clearly so the policeman could hear her. 'We were interviewed by Carmela Hernandez. Channel Five.'

Still silence. Then the voice barked out, 'You! Put your hands up.' The torch was directed at Alex.

Alex felt the beam like a searchlight on his body. He tried to remain calm. He put one hand up and raised the injured one as far as the sling would allow.

'You're the Indiana Jones guy who fought off the tomb robbers.'

Alex realized they were looking for his injury. 'That's right.'

The torch beam lowered and the voice became human. The loudhailer had been switched off. 'You can put your hands down. That's the high security area of the museum you're in. Why are you down there?'

Alex called out, 'We think we heard some of the children down here. We're worried they might have hidden here and got trapped.'

'There are injured people up there too,' said Li. 'Can you get medical help?'

'We'll do what we can,' said the policeman. 'But

it's chaos in the city. All the paramedics are busy. Shops are being looted. It's a state of emergency. Now we know you're here we'll try and send people your way, but I don't know how long it will be. Good luck.'

Footsteps crunched on the rubble as they receded.

They were alone again.

Señora Marquez let out her breath in a long, slow stream. 'I don't know how you guys knew what to do, but I think you saved our lives.'

Li looked at Alex. At least it sounded like the teacher trusted their judgement now. 'I think we'll be waiting a while before any official rescuers get here.'

'It's down to us then,' said Alex. 'Come on.'

'You know, I've never liked confined spaces,' said Hex. He had calmed down a little. His heart was no longer hammering like a bird trying to get out of his chest. He was going to be here for a while and he just had to accept it.

'I hate them,' said Susana. She spoke fast; anxiously. 'I never use lifts. I never go in narrow spaces on digs.'

She looked awful. Her face was wet in the glow from the light stick, her breathing shallow.

'What about the jungle?' said Hex.

She snapped at him. 'If you can't think of something else to talk about, shut up.'

Hex felt like he'd been slapped. He knew he wasn't good at small talk but he was only trying to make conversation to pass the time. He was about to answer back when a spasm crossed Susana's face and she closed her eyes.

Something was wrong. She had opened her eyes again, but they were staring and her breathing was fast.

She rubbed them and sighed loudly. 'Why don't they get us out?' She raised her voice to a shout. 'Hello? Can anybody hear me?'

There was no reply. Only the drip, drip of sand.

Hex was no medic; he had only basic first aid skills. He knew when to get help and what to do until it arrived, nothing more. This looked serious. In any other situation he'd have kept her warm and still and got her an ambulance.

She fidgeted, then collapsed back with the effort, breathing fast.

'Does it hurt?' he said. He felt helpless.

She half closed her eyes. Was she trying to think how to accurately describe her symptoms or was she just irritated?

'Have you got any water?' she said. 'I'm really thirsty.'

Hex shook his head. He couldn't even do that for her. I've got to get her talking about something else, he thought. That'll take her mind off it. Even if she doesn't want to.

'So you're not with the school?' he said.

The answer was snapped back at him. 'No. I work here.'

'What were you doing here?'

'I was working late. I went to sleep in my office. I have a deadline.' She moved and winced.

He remembered her then; coming out of her office as he climbed out of the dinosaur. If he hadn't called to her, made her come out, she might have been OK.

'Do something useful. Don't just lie there. Try that thing of yours, that computer.'

Hex got out his palmtop. He knew there was no point – but perhaps there was a point, he thought.

It might keep her happy. Plus, they had to fill the time until help arrived.

He powered up the little machine. Its screen cast a blue glow in the tiny space. It made the dinosaur bones around them more clear and real. He called up the e-mail program; it came up with the same message: no signal. The state-of-the-art machine was no more use than a games console. 'No,' he said. 'There's still nothing.' He put it away again carefully.

Susana let out an exasperated sigh and shivered. 'I'm parched. Have you got any water?'

Hex shook his head. She'd forgotten she'd just asked. It was a bit disturbing, as if her wiring had gone wrong.

All he had to do was keep her talking, keep her calm. Any minute now they might hear the chink-chink of pickaxes and then they could start getting out.

20 EVACUATION

Li climbed the fire hose that Paulo had left. They'd retraced their steps to just beyond where they'd hidden from the police, got into a small utility room that housed the main fuse boxes – and found a situation that was depressingly familiar. Jagged pieces of masonry filling the corridor. No spaces to squeeze through, and no sign of any space beyond. It was impassable. They listened but they heard nothing, just shifting masonry, as constant as the creak of rigging on a ship. The only positive point was that they'd been able to turn off the electricity properly. But it wasn't the rescue they were hoping for.

Li reached the top and began to thread the fire hose through the abseil harness. A sound made her pause.

A torch beam illuminated the front wall and there was a crunch of footsteps: someone was climbing through the hole.

The torch was too bright for Li to see who was holding it. The night vision goggles were still down at the bottom, with Alex and Señora Marquez. The light became steady, focused on the ground. Now the footsteps were coming towards her. She was about to call out but something about the figure made her skin prickle. It walked slowly, with assurance, as though completely used to that environment. Everyone else had been picking their way hesitantly. She saw a shadowy bulk. A man. A big man. He knew what he was doing and he moved with purpose.

A looter? Come to get the mask he'd seen on TV?

'Hello,' he called. His torch flashed over her, as if assessing her. Sizing her up to see how much trouble she'd be?

He loomed out of the darkness – a tall figure with

a thick neck. Li moved her feet surreptitiously. How firm was it underfoot? If she had to do a throw on him would she end up in the pit too?

He stopped beside Li and looked down at the makeshift abseil gear in her hands. She was getting ready to strike when a piercing voice came from the doorway of the axe room.

'Daddy!'

Beatriz was standing in the doorway with a light stick.

The man walked lightly across to her and picked her up in his strong arms. As he turned in the doorway there were more delighted shouts from the children in the room. Soon a scrum of small figures was attempting to hug him.

Li finished attaching the abseil harness, laughing quietly at herself. She was getting too jumpy.

Beatriz's father helped Li haul the others out of the basement and into what remained of the lobby. Soon Alex was in the axe room, where Paulo and Amber gave him a warm welcome.

'About time,' said Amber, looking him up and down.

'You lazy git,' said Paulo, slapping him playfully

on his good arm. 'What have you been doing all this time? Having a lie down?'

'Building up my strength, biding my time,' grinned Alex.

But then it was back to work. There was still so much to be done. 'Did you find anyone down there?' said Paulo.

Li shook her head. 'It's blocked. We couldn't get through.'

Alex took something out of his pocket. 'I got this. It was on the wall in the utility room.' He unfolded a big piece of paper.

Beatriz's father knew what it was immediately. 'Firemen's plans.'

Alex nodded. 'We should be able to find another way into those inaccessible places.'

'Are we going, Daddy?' Beatriz looked up at her father. 'Did you bring the van?'

He ruffled her hair. 'Yes, I did, and Mummy's outside waiting.' He turned to the four members of Alpha Force. 'I've got a van with blankets and medical supplies. It'll be a lot more comfortable and safer than staying in here.'

Paulo, Amber, Li and Alex looked at each other. 'Great – let's get organized. Are you from the emergency services?'

'Not exactly. Sorry, I'd better introduce myself. I used to be a fireman. Now I always make sure I've got equipment for emergencies because you never know when a disaster will happen. My name's Miguel.'

While they did the round of introductions, Li smiled to herself. Well that explained why he looked so comfortable walking into the wrecked building.

Señora Marquez had been quiet but she recognized the cue to swing into action. Clapping her hands for attention, she addressed the room in confident classroom tones. 'Girls and boys, listen up. We're going to be moving out of here so I want you to form a queue here by me.'

The children obediently lined up next to their teacher: Rosa, Gabriel, Pedro, Consuela, Beatriz, and two more who had recently been dug out – Sofia and Andreas. Vicente and Alejandro were out too; Paulo had been keeping a close eye on the boy and once he was warm and calm it was clear he was not injured.

Amber thought of the teacher under the rubble.

'If you guys go with the evacuation I'll stay with Señora Zapata, make sure she's OK.'

Señora Marquez caught the mention of her colleague's name and gave Amber a challenging look. Paulo took her elbow and said to her quietly, 'Your colleague is injured and can't get out, but we're looking after her.'

She looked torn for a moment, then professionalism took over. She glanced at the group of children in front of her. 'Are all the children you've freed here?'

Paulo admired her focus. She was doing her duty and putting the children first. Friends would have to wait until later.

'Put your light stick in your right hand and hug the wall as you go along,' called Miguel. The children were in a line, ready to embark on the tricky walk out of the building.

'I'll go first,' said Li.

Miguel had been about to volunteer to lead the way, but something about Li's confidence made him stand down. 'I'll bring up the rear,' he said.

Li trained her torch on the ground at her feet and

moved forwards. With the number of light sticks, the area was now bathed in a bright glow and Miguel could see what had been concealed when he came in with just a torch. All that was left of the floor was a ledge one metre wide. A lot of people would have been unnerved by the thought of being so close to a big drop but Li was walking along it as calmly as if it was a pavement on the edge of a road. It was a while since Miguel had worked in the fire service, but some of his colleagues had never achieved the level of coolness under pressure that he was seeing in Li.

And it was having a beneficial effect on everybody. Her certainty communicated itself to the rest of the party. Gabriel was right behind her, following quietly and sensibly. Then came Jose; then Rosa. Imelda followed her, then Sofia. Each child had an adult nearby to reassure them. Señora Marquez was next, followed by Consuela. Then came Alex, who was followed by Vicente. Paulo came after that, carrying Pedro because of his injured foot. Alejandro came next, and Andreas. Finally, Miguel brought up the rear, with Beatriz grasping his hand tightly.

Li's torch skimmed over the ragged hole left by

the girder. She peered through, then turned and took Gabriel's hand. 'Just climb through and wait on the other side.'

He climbed through and Li heard a woman's voice greet him. One by one, Li ushered the children through the hole and out of the dangerous building. When it was Paulo's turn, he lifted Pedro through and Jose helped him out on the other side.

Miguel stepped through with the three members of Alpha Force. A small, neat woman was guiding the children towards a white van parked next to a fallen tree.

'Come and meet my wife, Thalia,' said Miguel.

The road was deserted, eerily empty, but there was a wail of emergency sirens. The sky was dark except for occasional flashes of blue in the distance as ambulances and fire trucks fought through the streets.

'Listen to those sirens,' said Paulo. 'The city must be in chaos.' He flicked his torch back at the museum building; it caught the ragged hole they had climbed through, the render flaking off the walls like crumbling icing.

Alex was nodding. 'But we've got these kids out.'

'Four more to go – and Señora Zapata,' said Li. 'And Hex.'

Amber stuck her head into the little hole. 'How are you doing?'

'Fine,' said Señora Zapata. But she didn't sound fine, she sounded worried.

'Are you in any pain?' said Amber.

The teacher shook her head. 'No, I'm all right.' She smiled at Amber weakly. 'Isn't it quiet, now the children have gone? I thought you were all leaving me.'

'We wouldn't do that.' Amber crawled into the small space and made herself comfortable. The area under the concrete slab was different now; frightening and bleak without the sound of the children's steady chatter and the glow from their light sticks. How horrible to be trapped in here, unable to move.

'Have you found everyone?' asked the teacher.

'Most of them,' said Amber. 'Four of the children still haven't been seen.'

'I know there's someone dead under that rock over there.'

Amber was stunned. They'd tried to keep that from everyone. 'How did you know?'

'When you've got nothing to do you notice a lot of things. Jose and Imelda – and you and that big good-looking friend of yours kept the kids away. It's my colleague Señor Mermoz, isn't it?'

Amber nodded.

'I knew something must have happened to him. Normally he'd have been out here organizing everyone. He's a big personality. You notice when he's in the room and you also notice when he's not.' Her hands were clasped together, the fingers fidgeting. The pads of her fingers were free of dust, unlike the rest of her hands. She looked like she'd been doing a lot of worrying.

The teacher sighed. 'My husband wanted to come on this trip, but he had to visit his mother. She's not well. I'm glad he didn't come; to get trapped in this. But I'm also worried I'll never see him again.'

'He might have got out,' said Amber. 'Don't lose hope.'

'I don't mean him,' said Señora Zapata. 'He phoned me just after the quake hit. He was all right

– he's on his way.' She drew her hands apart. In the glow from the light stick Amber saw something glint. 'When he comes, will you give this to him?'

It was a small circle of gold. A wedding ring. Amber was shocked. 'Oh no, that's not necessary. Listen, let me get you some water—'

Señora Zapata cut her off. 'Amber, I know why they haven't freed me. They can't. They daren't. They said they need to wait for the ambulance. But when is an ambulance going to get through? Jose said the roads are blocked. No one's going anywhere. How long can I stay like this? I can't feel my legs.'

Amber took a deep breath. She also took the ring and slid it gently back onto the woman's finger. 'Señora Zapata, you're right that we can't move you. But you're still alive and we're still fighting for you.'

Señora Zapata closed her eyes and folded her hands one on top of the other. She looked serene, like an effigy on top of a tomb. 'You're right. I shouldn't give up hope. You're not giving up hope.'

Amber caught the tone in her voice. 'No,' she agreed quietly. 'We're not giving up hope.'

* * *

Li, Paulo, Alex, Jose and Miguel returned to the ruined museum and made their way back in along the ledge. Jose had the sledgehammer; Miguel had a crowbar. Li and Paulo had light sticks and torches. They had left Thalia, Imelda and Señora Marquez with the children, giving out blankets and hot drinks from water boiled on a camping stove.

'We'll look at the fire plans,' said Miguel. 'In such a big building there should be another way into that basement, perhaps from outside.'

Li stopped. 'Don't move,' she said.

Unquestioningly, Paulo and Alex obeyed her. Miguel did too. These kids really worked together as a team, he thought. They were like a tight-knit military unit.

'What's up?' said Paulo.

'I felt something,' said Li. 'Something moved.'

They all felt the sweat freeze on their backs. Was it another tremor? An aftershock?

Very, very tentatively, Alex put his hand on the wall.

It was vibrating.

He yelled, 'Outside!'

They turned like lightning and ran for the hole in

the wall. They dived out, rolled on the ground and in moments were on their feet and running away across the cracked paving stones.

Paulo called out. 'Stop, guys. It's not a quake.' He stood and bent over, getting his breath. The others looked at him as though he was mad. 'The ground's not shaking,' he gasped.

Li and Alex looked at each other. 'I definitely felt something move,' said Li.

'So did I,' said Miguel.

From inside the building there was a crash. The four observers threw themselves to the ground. The shocks reverberated through their bones. Screams came from Miguel's white van.

Slowly, Alex looked up. Then Paulo. Then Li and Miguel.

Alex flashed the torch over the building. It looked the same but there had been so much damage already that spotting anything new was difficult.

It was Li who noticed. 'It's the roof. Another section's fallen in.'

Miguel sighed. 'Must have been weakened.'

'And Amber's still in there,' said Alex.

21 DYING WISH

Hex heard a crash. He tried to sit up but the thump of solid masonry against his elbows, spine and knees reminded him that he couldn't move. But what was that sound?

He realized he hadn't heard any sounds from outside in ages.

'Did you hear that?'

'What?' snapped Susana.

'I heard something. Ssh.'

It didn't come again. The only sound he could hear was Susana's breathing.

She slumped back against the uncomfortable surface. 'I didn't hear anything.' She tried to shift position but froze as if she'd been jabbed painfully. For a moment she lay like that and panted. Her breath was like steam in the tiny space. Hex could feel it on his face, his hands. 'I need to get out of here. Can't you do something?'

No, he couldn't. That was the really difficult part. All the time he'd been in Alpha Force he'd been able to do things. Now he just had to sit here and wait for help. 'They'll get to us soon,' he said.

Susana fidgeted again, trying to find a new position, but she always came back to the same one. 'Did you hear something or not? It's a simple question.'

Hex tried to remember. He thought he'd heard something fall. But now it was the same as before – the never-changing trickle of small pieces of rubble cascading down through the cracks between the bones. The sudden noise seemed like a figment of his imagination.

'What was it? People?'

'Yes, I think so.' It was better to believe that than not to believe it. A story he'd once heard popped into his head. Imagine a tree in a big, big wood. If it fell and no one was there to hear it, did it make a noise?

He looked down at his hand. Ants were running over it. The rubble was teeming with them. Some of them were carrying things – small pieces of debris, wood, each piece almost the size of the ant's body. If I was as strong as an ant, thought Hex, I could lift these bones and get out. But human beings were so fragile.

Susana kept fidgeting. She struck her hand against one of the bones as though she could bat it out of the way. 'God, I'm thirsty. Have you got any water?'

That question again. Her brain was going round and round in big, ratty circles. What was it that was wrong with her? Was she about to have some kind of epileptic fit? What would he do if she did?

'Look,' he said. 'Do you have any medical problems I should know about?' She glared at him and he added, 'If you're asleep when they come to get us out I may have to tell them.'

'No,' she retorted. 'I'm just cold and thirsty and I've got the worst indigestion ever.' She coughed. Wet breath hit his face again.

Her lips looked black in the fluorescent green light; her skin white and clammy. She looked like a vampire. He wiped her breath off his cheek. When he took his hand away there was blood on it.

Amber's instincts took over. She heard the bang and suddenly she was like a gecko, running along the ground as fast as possible, keeping low, protecting herself. The light stick was in her fist but she didn't know where she was going.

Behind her there was a crash that she felt through her bones. She hit the deck and rolled into a ball, her hands clasped tightly over her head. Masonry fell. Oh God, it was happening again.

When it stopped, Amber was ready for the rumbling, but this time the ground beneath her knees and elbows was still. Solid.

A shaft of light pierced through the gloom. White light. From a torch. She raised her head.

'Amb-er!' It was Alex's voice.

She got to her feet as the others piled in. They checked her carefully as she brushed herself down. 'Ow!' She bent double and clutched her leg in pain.

'What's wrong?' said Li, and knelt down to look.

'It's all right, it's just my bite,' said Amber. 'It's been hurting all night.'

They flashed the torches around the room, looking at the wreckage. A concrete beam had come down, right where Amber had been lying with Señora Zapata. The great table of concrete had smashed to smithereens. Amber had managed to crawl about thirty metres in less than a few seconds.

Amber turned to look at Paulo. 'I left Señora Zapata there.'

'Señora Zapata?' called Paulo.

There was no answer.

Li turned to the ex fireman. 'Miguel, do you think it's safe to go and investigate?'

Miguel looked up at the roof. A big section was missing. They could see the flashes of blue in the sky from far-off emergency vehicles. 'Hard to tell.'

Li gave him the night vision goggles. 'Try these.'

Miguel lifted them to his eyes. He inspected the wrecked joists, the ragged end of the concrete beam. 'Yes, it looks stable. But there's a body over there.'

Li took the goggles from him. The debris covering

Señor Mermoz had slipped away. His spectacles were smashed, the empty frames filled like egg-cups with dust and glass.

Li looked at him for longer than she'd intended to. She saw the glowing forms of Paulo and Amber as they passed in front of the goggles to look for Señora Zapata. By comparison, Señor Mermoz looked faded, not vibrant white. This was what a body looked like when it was cold.

She looked at Amber and Paulo. They were on their hands and knees, gently pulling away debris. Beyond, she could see Señora Zapata's bright chest. A pool of brilliant white was seeping out from the pile of concrete. She realized what it was. Blood. Fresh, warm blood.

Paulo and Amber had stopped. Li took the goggles off and walked quietly up to them. 'Do you need these?'

Paulo shook his head. He was shining his torch at Señora Zapata. Straight in her eyes. They were open and she wasn't flinching.

Señora Zapata looked peaceful, but that was only from one side. A piece of concrete had hit her head and made her skull a shape it shouldn't be. It was smashed in along one side. Blood framed her head like a dark halo. A clear liquid was running out of her nose and left ear. Cerebrospinal fluid; the fluid that circulates through the brain and spinal cord. She must have died instantly.

Amber looked at Paulo, tears in her eyes. They had tried to keep her alive, but now the roof had collapsed and killed her anyway. Paulo reached forward and gently ran his hand down the woman's face. Her eyes closed.

Amber took her hand. The ring was still there, where she'd put it back less than half an hour ago. She could feel the bones inside the flesh. 'She said her husband was on his way. She asked me to give him her ring.'

Slowly, she slid the circle of metal off the woman's finger.

Paulo spoke in Li's ear. 'Is there anyone else in here? You can see with those goggles.'

Li stood up and scanned the room. 'No. It's clear.'

Alex spotted a familiar shape leaning up next to a tall vase. His bergen. He went up to it, brushed the dust off and opened the top.

Paulo looked at Li in disbelief. The bergen had survived yet again.

Alex began stuffing items into his belt kit. 'Thanks for looking after it.'

'We haven't,' said Paulo. 'But someone must have.'

'Shall we just all get in it in case anything else happens?' Li asked.

Miguel had the fireman's plans. 'Let's get out, grab some coffee and take a good look at these.'

Susana coughed again. The blood collected in dark gobbets around her mouth, as though she had been eating black fruit. Her breathing was shallow and fast and she was shivering, even though it was sweltering inside the tiny space.

'Hex, have you ever thought you were going to die?'

She hadn't talked for a while. She seemed to be thinking; thinking up difficult questions and then hitting him with them. 'Yes. I have.'

'What was it like?'

How many times? Since he'd met Amber and the others, too many to count. Nothing like this, though. Or no, wait a minute. They had been cave diving on a mission in Alaska: he had followed Amber around a tight bend in a tunnel and got stuck. But that had been different. Amber knew what to do and got him out.

He wished he hadn't thought about that time diving in the cave. He remembered that feeling of a huge mass of rock above him, and him trapped and squirming. Except this was worse. He and Susana had been spared because when the bones fell they had left this little gap, but would it hold for ever?

For ever . . . ?

'When did you nearly die?'

No, he didn't want to revisit it. It wouldn't do any good. 'I didn't really,' he said to Susana. He changed the subject. 'My friends have got the latest thermal imaging equipment. They'll be searching for trapped people and they'll see us.'

Inside his head, he gave himself a different answer. No one had come yet. What if the others were trapped too? Or worse, he and Susana might be the sole survivors. Who would know to look for them?

Susana sighed; it was loud, full of pain. He felt he should do something. He put a hand on her forehead.

She twitched away from him, but it must have hurt her because she grimaced and went rigid. He couldn't do anything for her.

'I don't want to die,' she said. 'Not here, like this. I won't even have a gravestone. I'll have just disappeared. What about my family? They won't know if I'm dead or not. My mum and dad don't live in Belize City. They're probably perfectly all right—' Her sentence ended in more coughing. Mucus and blood blew out of her mouth like bubblegum. Her face was wet with tears.

A tree in a wood with no one to hear it fall.

Hex took her hand. 'Shh. Someone will be here soon.'

'Your friends with the imager?'

The goggles couldn't do that much. Only Superman could see through this much rubble; real-life technology wasn't that advanced. 'Yes, they'll be here soon. They'll get us out.' He had never told such a lie in his entire life.

Li, Amber, Alex, Paulo, Jose and Miguel walked across the grass. They had identified an entrance to the basement levels at the far end of the building. They passed the dinosaur gallery. The front wall had caved in; the roof looked like a giant wrecking ball had crashed into it.

'*Dios*,' said Paulo. 'This has really been battered.'

'Miguel,' said Amber, 'have you dealt with an earthquake before?'

Miguel nodded. 'A long time ago. And other big catastrophes. There was a big fire a few years ago where a hundred people died. I was injured. That's when I was pensioned out.'

'How long do you carry on looking?' said Li. 'When do you decide you have to stop?'

'That's really hard,' said Miguel. 'You never think you've done enough.'

'Well, it's different today,' said Paulo. 'We know how many we're looking for. Four children and Hex.'

They had reached the end of the building. A few metres from the corner was a fire door. They went closer and Alex played his torch over it. 'Hmm – look at this.' The glass had been smashed but the wire cage inside it had held the fragments together. It had been jemmied open from the outside. The wooden frame was splintered and a gouge showed pale like a wound. 'Looks like someone's already been in.'

'Might be other rescuers,' said Jose.

Alex and Li exchanged glances. They had a bad feeling.

By now the routine for entering a new area was established. Paulo, Alex and Miguel inspected the stairwell with the light from their torches; Alex viewed it through the night vision goggles. It was dusty and there were cracks in the walls, but the stairwell was fairly intact. They listened. Any cries? Any sounds of movement?

Nothing. It was quiet.

'I think we can go in,' said Miguel.

Alex led the way down to basement level, then they stopped to take stock. Amber got out the plans. They showed a main corridor leading to a set of small offices. 'According to this, it's a bit of a warren down here.'

Paulo looked into the gloom of the corridor. 'I wonder how much of it is still standing.' He flashed his torch in. It looked practically untouched; there wasn't even any dust – as if it had missed the quake entirely. 'Corridor looks OK.'

There was a muffled sound, like a trapped animal. Paulo looked round.

Everyone had heard it. 'Hello?' called Miguel. 'Shout again. Where are you?'

They got an answer. High-pitched squealing, like bats.

Alex shouted out loudly, 'Keep calling. We're coming.'

They padded carefully along the corridor. Miguel sounded a warning note: 'This looks OK but be prepared to take cover if something starts moving.'

The cries were getting louder. 'There's definitely more than one,' said Li.

They came to a door. Li pushed it gently and it swung open. 'Hello?'

'Here! Help!'

Alex looked into the room with the goggles. His hopes turned to fears. The ceiling had fallen in: the voices were coming from a pile of rubble on the floor.

Then he saw two glowing fingers appear in the middle of the debris. 'There!'

Li got down on her hands and knees and shone her torch into the hole where the fingers were poking through.

Three pairs of eyes blinked back. 'Hi there,' said Li. 'Is anyone hurt?'

Three voices chorused, 'No.'

'Miguel,' said Li, 'we need your expert opinion.'

She stood back. Miguel bent down and shone his torch in. 'Hi, girls. Let's just see where you've managed to end up—'

'I'm a boy!' said a voice crossly.

'Sorry,' said Miguel. He stood up. 'They're in a box of some kind. Must have got under a desk. Mind out.' He put the crowbar in the hole and pulled.

Several lumps of masonry tumbled out. A second go and the space was big enough for the children to crawl through.

Paulo, Li and Amber helped them out. Two girls and a boy stepped carefully over the rubble and blinked at the torches. Alex took the goggles off and put them back in their case. Best to conserve power, just in case.

Paulo watched the children carefully, looking to

see how they moved. They were shaken and dusty, but looked unhurt. Would he ever be able to meet anyone again without checking them for injuries?

'What are your names?' said Amber.

'Ana.'

Amber grinned. 'Ana Gomez, right?' The distinctive eyes and nose were a giveaway. They'd found one of Felipe's children. Ana nodded.

'I'm Toni Velázquez,' said the other girl.

'Roberto Cortes,' said the boy.

'Ana, where's Jorges?' asked Amber.

'We don't know,' replied Ana. 'We were looking for him. I woke up and he wasn't here. I thought he'd gone to the loo. I went to find him and Roberto and Toni came with me. Then the floor fell in. We landed in this room.'

Alex was investigating their hiding place. It was a big steel safe, like a chest freezer on its side, empty except for their footprints. 'You chose the right place to take cover. How did you get it open?'

'A rock fell on top of it and the door burst open. We thought it was a good place to hide. Then it got buried and we couldn't get out at all.'

Alex grinned at them. 'Did you find any jewels in there?'

'There was a mask,' said Ana. 'That big gold mask . . .'

The four members of Alpha Force looked at each other.

'You're Indiana Jones!' exclaimed Toni, although it wasn't clear which of them she was addressing.

Then Roberto spotted Alex's sling too. 'You got hurt fighting the tomb robber. Wow – can I see?'

'It's nothing,' shrugged Alex.

Li swept her torch around the rubble in front of them. 'Where's the mask now?'

'A man came and took it,' said Ana.

'A man took it?' repeated Paulo.

'We were stuck in here and someone came into the room,' said Ana. 'He seemed to be looking for people, like you were. We shouted. He took no notice. We thought he couldn't hear us. So we got the mask through the hole and waved it to get atten-tion. He came up and took it, then went away, leaving us.'

'The jemmied fire door,' said Li. 'There have

been looters in here. Remember the police?'

'Cool,' said Roberto. 'Are you going to fight them off?'

'No,' said Amber sternly. 'We are going to get you to safety. We've got warm blankets upstairs and your friends are waiting.'

Automatically, the four members of Alpha Force formed a protective formation to walk the kids out to the surface. Alex and Amber went in front; Paulo and Li were behind. Miguel led the way with the crowbar; Jose brought up the rear.

'Then will you come back and fight them off?' said Roberto.

'We'll come back and find Jorges,' said Li. 'And a friend of ours who's missing.'

Susana started to jerk. She looked as though she was trying to sit up but something inside her was broken.

Hex put his hands on her shoulders. 'Shh, shh. Don't try to move.' He didn't know what else to do. But she wouldn't keep still. It was like something inside her was moving her against her will.

He heard rasping sounds in her throat.

'Do you want to turn over?' he said. 'Shall I help you?'

She couldn't answer – just went on jerking. Her hands were picking at her chest and abdomen as though trying to get rid of something.

Was she trying to be sick? She might choke. He wasn't sure what to do.

'Susana, I'm going to move you. You should be more comfortable.' He took her shoulders and tried to turn her.

She screamed and he let go. He'd better not try again.

Her lips were blue and parched, her eyes half-closed and dull, the lids flickering. Around her mouth blood had crusted. It looked black in the light of the fluorescent stick.

Then she was still. The fit must have passed. The only sound in the tiny cavern was her breathing. It made a bubbling sound. She was hardly a person any more. Just a body gone wrong.

Her lips were moving. She was trying to speak. Hex leaned closer and put his ear to her mouth. He felt the wet breath on it and felt her blood spraying out over him.

The hot breath rasped and stopped. Her head lolled. The hands flopped down and were still.

For a moment Hex sat back and just looked at her. Slowly he reached for her wrist and felt for a pulse.

He couldn't find one. He tried again; even checked on his own wrist to make sure he'd got the right place.

There was no pulse.

Her eyes were still half open, looking at him. But instead of darting around they were still. Dead still.

He looked at his watch: 3.45 a.m. That was meant to be important, wasn't it? Time of death? Someone might want to know what time she died.

Now he was alone.

22 THE RING

Amber, Alex and Miguel came out of the fire door at the side of the building. They had sent Li, Paulo, Jose and the children on ahead while they searched the toilets. Both sets had survived, apart from flooding, but Jorges was not there. In the distance Miguel's van looked inviting – interior light on; children sitting inside, wrapped in blankets. Outside, Imelda and Señora Marquez were standing next to a camping stove pouring out coffee or talking to parents. It almost looked like a normal social gathering – except for the wrecked museum visible in the torchlight.

Amber was downcast. 'Jorges must have gone somewhere else.'

Alex tried to keep his voice positive. 'We've found all the other kids. We're going to find him too.'

'He might be anywhere,' said Miguel. 'You'd be surprised what little nooks and crannies these kids can get into.'

A figure came up to them. 'Excuse me?'

Amber saw Miguel's hand tighten around the crow bar.

'Have you seen my wife? She's a teacher. Señora Zapata.'

Miguel relaxed. Amber swallowed. The husband of the dead teacher. She put her hand on Alex's good arm. 'Give me five minutes. I'll catch up with you guys.'

Alex and Miguel became silhouettes as they carried on walking towards the van. Amber took Señor Zapata gently by the arm and slowed him down so they could have some privacy.

The man was nervous. He started talking. 'I've been walking for hours. Everywhere it's the same. Destroyed.'

Amber let him talk. It was as though he'd been

storing up fears for hours and had to let them out.

'But people keep being rescued. I met two men who were coming here too. They were looking for their children. We laughed and said, if we got out, our kids will have got out too. Children are tougher than men. Women are tougher than men.'

Amber's heart wrenched. It was like he was pleading with her not to tell him the news that he dreaded.

But she had to. 'I'm afraid she died,' she said gently.

He said nothing. Just stood as if unplugged.

What else should she say? Should she let him ask the next question? She remembered what it was like when she was told that her parents had died. Her uncle had broken the news. She remembered that he had let her ask questions when she was ready. Don't rush him, she thought. Let him be in charge.

Finally he asked, 'How did it happen?'

What should she say? Your wife's legs were crushed. We didn't find her for hours. We decided moving her would kill her, but because we didn't move her she died when the roof fell in. Amber felt miserably ashamed. They had all failed. No, get a grip, she told herself. He has a right to know what happened. Our guilt is nothing to do with it. Be as honest as possible.

Amber swallowed hard. 'She was trapped when a wall fell down. She wasn't in any pain but we couldn't get her out. Then the roof suddenly collapsed and it killed her instantly.'

Señor Zapata was nodding, but he looked as if he couldn't take it in. 'Thank you,' he said.

Why thank me? thought Amber. I don't know if I did the right thing.

'Were you with her?' he said.

Amber nodded. 'Yes.' She desperately wanted to say something comforting – she told me about you, she seemed so brave, the children went and kept her company. But Amber had hardly known the woman; anything she said seemed hollow.

Then she had another thought. What if he asked to see the body? Should she take him into the dangerous building and show him his wife with her head smashed in? Show him how she'd spent her final few hours? Should she tell him a white lie to spare him that sight?

Amber remembered something. At last. This was something she could do. She put her fingers in her pocket and brought out Señora Zapata's wedding ring.

Señor Zapata took it and looked at it in silence. It was as if the whole world was contained in that circle of gold.

'Thank you,' he said eventually, as if he'd only just remembered someone was there.

He didn't want anyone else around. He didn't want to ask any more questions. Amber patted him on the shoulder and left him.

As she walked away to join the others, her eyes were blurred with tears. She didn't see the man who had been watching them.

Hex moved the light stick away from the body. Not that there was much room in the hole, but he didn't want to see it. He put the light stick into a little crevice. At eye level? No, that dazzled him and made the hole seem smaller. He wiggled it into another cranny. That was better. He was side on to it now. And he could turn away from the body so he didn't have to look at it.

He heard a creak. Something was moving.

Was that someone coming to rescue him?

'Hello?' he called. Then he listened hard. So hard he could hear his own nervous system sing.

It didn't come again.

Were the bones shifting? Had they been making this noise before or was this new? Were they about to come crashing down and claim this space occupied by two soft bodies?

Nothing happened. The sound didn't come again. It must have been one of those creaks, like you get in a house as it settles. There was just the gentle scraping of sand, trickling down, down, down between the bones.

They were like fossils in a rock wall, sandwiched between concrete and these fossilized dinosaur bones. One day they'd be found, fossils in fossils. No one would know that he'd been the last one to die. In the general scale of fossil time, millions of years, that was irrelevant. He looked at his watch again. Barely fifteen minutes since Susana had died. Fifteen minutes since he'd heard another voice. And already it seemed an age.

He turned on his palmtop. There was still no signal; a blank box where normally he would expect to see how many satellites could see him, how strong the signal was, how many e-mails he'd got. He tried not to look at the box. Its blankness said, No one can see you. You are alone.

He brought up a text editor. Having his fingers on the keys was good. For just a moment it made these looming walls disappear.

What would he write?

His fingers were ahead of his brain. He found he'd had already typed the first line. He read it out loud. That helped. That made it like really talking.

'Dear Amber.'

Amber caught up with the others at Miguel's van. Li gave her a bagel. 'From Imelda. All the power was off in their house so she brought the contents of her fridge along.'

The last thing Amber felt like was eating, but she knew she should. Automatically she took a bite and chewed. Her stomach seemed to turn somersaults of delight, but eating seemed like it was part of another world. The old world. Before the quake.

Alex brought coffees and handed one to Paulo and one to Amber. 'We'll have to go back in and do a proper search for Jorges and Hex.'

Li, beside him, nodded. 'We should get all the light sticks we can, all the torches we can, all the tools.'

'I'll see if I can get any of the children to part with their light sticks,' said Paulo, going towards the van.

'By the way, Felipe's here,' said Li. 'He walked across town. He said it was bedlam. Looting, collapsed buildings.'

'I'm worried about these looters,' said Amber. 'Do you think Jorges is in any danger from them?'

'Shouldn't think so,' said Alex. 'They're not interested in hurting people. They just want things they can sell.'

Far off, they heard the call of sirens. It had barely stopped all night.

'Hex must be wondering where we've got to,' said Li.

'I wonder what's happened to him?'

'Lazy lout,' said Amber. 'He's probably playing

games on his palmtop in a nice quiet spot somewhere.'

'Yeah,' said Alex. 'When it runs out of batteries we'll see him quickly enough.'

They saw Paulo coming back, illuminated like a floodlit statue by an armful of light sticks. He put them on the ground in a big glowing pile. 'These should make things a bit easier,' he said.

Li looked at him severely. 'I don't believe you stole the children's light sticks. How the fabric of society breaks down at a time like this.'

Alex was looking into the distance. 'Who's that? Is it Señor Zapata?' He pointed. Near the trees, a figure was wandering into the night.

'That's not him,' said Amber. 'I don't know who that is.'

As they watched, the man started running. He disappeared into a darkened area. Then they heard blows. The unmistakable sound of somebody being attacked.

Amber, Paulo, Li and Alex gave chase.

Alex's torch picked out Señor Zapata, sitting on the ground, dazed. The other man had attacked him and was running away.

The others raced past, pursuing the attacker, as Alex stopped beside Señor Zapata and helped him to his feet. 'Are you all right?'

The man's voice shook. 'I didn't know he was there. He took my wife's ring.'

Alex looked up. Three torches converged on the running man like cross-hairs on a target. 'We'll get it back, don't you worry.'

The man was a good runner, but Amber, Li and Paulo were trained to peak condition.

Paulo was so close that his torch picked out the pattern on the man's shirt. Ahead were trees – he was running into a wood. Amber, Li and Paulo hared in after him. Branches crashed underfoot.

Li saw a chance. She leaped up, grabbed a branch and swung towards the fleeing man. Her legs caught him around the neck in a scissors action and a moment later he was on the ground. He struggled, but Li got on top of him and twisted his arm up behind his neck. He cried out and stopped struggling. Li smiled, kneeling on his back. 'Yeah, you keep still and you'll find it doesn't hurt as much.'

'He's ready for you,' Li told Amber and Paulo.

Still holding the man, she pulled him upright into a kneeling position.

Amber strolled up to him and put her hand out. 'Give me the ring, scumbag.'

The man spat at her. Li tightened her hold and his gesture ended in an agonized cry.

'The ring,' said Paulo.

Amber was so tempted to kick the man. It would have been easy. A good boot in the solar plexus was just what he deserved for robbing a bereaved man.

'Look in his pockets,' said Paulo. He bent down and put his fingers into the man's jeans pocket. The man gave him a murderous look but Li kept him obedient.

Paulo pulled out the ring. 'Thank you,' he said graciously.

Li got off the man's back and gave another tweak. 'On your feet. And don't try anything.'

The man got up. Paulo took his other arm and they began to walk him back to the others.

Alex and Señor Zapata, accompanied by Miguel, met them at the edge of the wood.

'There's a police van over there,' said Miguel.

'They're questioning Ana, Roberto and Toni about the looters they saw. I think they'll be very interested in our friend here.' He took the mugger by the arm; the man looked at him malevolently and Miguel clapped a pair of handcuffs on him. 'Nice catch, by the way,' he said. He turned his captive round and escorted him away.

Amber gave the ring to Señor Zapata. 'Be careful who sees this,' she said.

Señor Zapata nodded. 'Thank you,' he said quietly and started to walk slowly towards the lighted van.

'He looks so lost,' murmured Paulo.

They all watched him for a long moment.

The four friends walked back to where the light sticks still stood in a glowing pile.

Alex handed them out. 'Come on. Work to do. People to rescue.'

'Hey,' said Amber, 'this isn't a very good one. Are they all like this?' The stick in her hands was no longer bright and luminous; its light was feeble.

'This one's a bit better,' said Alex. He held his alongside Amber's. It was brighter but not brilliant. As he compared the two Amber's faded completely.

'They only last eight hours,' said Paulo quietly. 'They must be running out.'

'These are going too,' said Li. In moments the sticks she was holding were useless dark tubes.

They looked at the dulling sticks in silence. It seemed like a graphic warning.

Alex remembered the TV interview; how they'd both stood at the edges of the group shot, trying to sneak out. He saw Hex's mocking look as the camera zoomed in on Alex's heroic injury.

Paulo remembered Hex somehow managing to get a hammock to himself so that he and Alex were forced to share. He remembered him in the heli, absorbed in his palmtop, off in his own little world. He was such a private person. Always so protective of his space – both external and internal. *Amigo*, he said to himself, I hope you're protecting yourself very well right now.

Li remembered the last time she'd seen him, by the dinosaur. They thought they'd knocked it over. They were laughing with relief at the ridiculous idea of putting it back together. Then the world had changed.

Amber tried to remember the last thing she'd said to Hex. She couldn't. And suddenly she couldn't picture his face either. Just looking down from the heli as they came into land in Belize City; the markings on the tarmac became a clearing in the jungle with a flaming H, where five friends danced, shouted and capered at the end of another mad expedition.

Hex watched as the light stick faded. First it dimmed, like a temporary glitch in mains power. But it didn't come back on.

His world shrank. The only thing he could see now was the screen of his palmtop. The space around him became bluish. Cold.

How cold it had got. Of course. Susana's body had stopped giving out heat. Hex shivered.

There was no air. How long had he been breathing this same air? He put his hands to his throat. He felt like he was suffocating. Was that what would get him?

He coughed, and then he couldn't stop. There was so much dust. All that pulverized bone. All that sand trickling incessantly. Soon he would be breathing sand. The air would run out and he would drown in sand.

Could he still smell things? He sniffed the air, his skin. Surely his sweat must smell. Nothing. His senses were being dulled, like the light stick. Shutting down.

What was the last sense to go? Was it smell? No, it was hearing. Well, there was nothing to hear.

He moved the screen of the palmtop around, trying to use it as a torch. Even that wouldn't last for ever. The batteries would go. He knew every shadow so well by now. That bulge that was the remains of the T. rex's humerus. That pale oval in the corner was Susana's face. He should have turned it towards the wall so it couldn't look at him. But he didn't want to touch it now.

He hadn't written anything more for about five minutes now. He'd said all he wanted to say. All the palmtop was now was a torch. It showed how tiny the space was.

He whispered, 'I think I prefer the dark.'

He turned the palmtop off.

23 UNDERWORLD

Amber, Paulo, Li and Alex had spread the plans on the bonnet of the van.

'Where haven't we searched yet?' said Alex.

A word on the plan suddenly leaped out at Paulo like a neon sign. WORKSHOP.

Miguel brought Felipe over. They'd got two pick-axes as well as Miguel's crowbar.

'Felipe,' said Paulo decisively. 'We know where to look for Jorges.'

'Oh yes?' said Li.

Felipe looked at him. His eyes were full of hope and anxiety. 'Where?'

'He's gone to see the animatronic dinosaur in the workshop.'

Felipe hit his forehead with the heel of his hand. 'Of course! He was angling to see it last night.'

Paulo gestured to him. 'It's your territory. Lead the way.'

Alex had the night vision goggles and his belt pack. Paulo had the makeshift first-aid kit. Li and Amber had torches – as did Felipe and Miguel. They walked back into the building with purpose. This was a positive lead – someone else they could get out. Maybe at some point they'd get a lead for Hex.

Felipe took them down the fire escape to the basement. When they reached the small office with the fallen ceiling, he gasped. 'Ana was under that? It's a miracle they got out alive.'

Amber patted his arm. 'They were clever. The safe burst open and Ana got them in for protection. Hopefully Jorges will be clever too.'

Miguel was impressed. Amber instinctively understood they had to keep the man's morale up.

Felipe took them past another office and peered

in. 'It's not too bad in there,' he said. But it was empty, so he continued to the next one.

A little further on he stopped. His torch flashed on a heap of rubble. It went from floor to ceiling, like a roughly built wall. 'Jesus,' he said in a low voice. 'The workshop is just through there. The T. rex must have crashed through the floor. It weighs tonnes.'

'We can't get through there,' said Li.

'Alex, have you got the plans?' said Miguel. 'With all these little rooms we might be able to knock a way through.'

Alex handed the plans over. Miguel tapped the map confidently. 'This side wall is a plasterboard partition. We should try knocking it down and see if there's a way in there.'

Paulo had a pickaxe ready. 'Where do you want the hole?'

Miguel pointed. 'About here, quite low down.' Amber and Li trained the torches on the area.

Paulo gripped the axe with both hands and swung. The point crashed into the wall. He hooked it out, leaving a ragged hole and a shower of dust. With the next blow he levered out a bigger piece.

Felipe let out a great long worried breath. Li put a reassuring hand on his arm. She understood what he felt. He was afraid of what he might find.

Amber took the other pickaxe and helped Paulo make the hole bigger.

Li crawled in, then stuck her head back again to report what she'd found. 'It's fine. Not much damage.'

Miguel consulted the map. 'OK, we go in there, then knock another hole through to the next room.'

The party squeezed through the opening and Miguel inspected the left-hand wall. 'Paulo, make a hole about here.'

Paulo lined up the axe. 'With pleasure.' He took a couple of big swings and Amber helped him enlarge the hole.

Li went through first. 'Clear,' she called.

Amber followed. Alex handed her the night vision goggles and climbed through, awkwardly because of his injured hand. Paulo followed, then Felipe, then finally Miguel.

'Hey, this is the kitchen,' said Li. Her torch picked out a steel sink, taps and a draining board. 'Anyone fancy a cup of tea?'

Miguel consulted the plans. 'The next wall to take out is' – he pointed – 'there.'

Amber flashed the torch over. 'You mean the one with the big hole in it?' Sure enough, there was a big hole like the one they'd made in the other wall.

'Felipe,' she asked, 'have you got a problem with rats here?'

Felipe was looking at the hole, tight lipped. 'Human rats. Looters.'

Amber played her torch over the walls. 'But how did they get in here? They didn't come down the fire escape. There must be another way out.'

Li bent down to step through the hole, but Alex stopped her. 'We'd better be careful. They might still be here. Take the goggles in case someone's hiding.'

Li handed her torch to Alex, then put the goggles on and stepped carefully through the hole.

On the other side was a bigger room, like a garage. To her left was a mass of rubble. To her right was a carved stone stele like the ones in the entrance, partly wrapped for transit – but nothing warm and breathing.

'All clear,' she called back.

The others came out carefully.

'Hey, Felipe,' she said, 'you've got one treasure left intact.'

Felipe put a hand on the stele and looked up into the beautiful stone face. 'That's on loan from Mexico City. I'm glad we don't have to tell them we broke it.'

Amber's voice called him back to reality. 'Felipe?'

They all turned. Leaning against the outside wall was a ladder. It led to a long dark hole like a letter box, just below the ceiling. Outside, it must be at ground level.

Felipe looked up the ladder. 'That was a window. We blocked it off for security reasons. Not that we ever thought anyone could get a stele out through it.'

Amber shone her torch on the ground. 'Well, someone's unblocked it.' A couple of breeze blocks lay broken on the dusty floor. 'Guys, we have to be very careful.'

Miguel was holding his torch over the plans. He spoke in a quiet voice. 'Were we looking for the workshop? Because it's there, where that pile of rubble is.'

The other torches converged on the wreckage.

Pieces of ceiling, chunks of wall from the floor above, formed an impenetrable mountain.

Felipe walked towards it with heavy steps. 'Jorges?' he called. 'Jorges?'

The whole room held its breath, waiting for a reply. There was nothing. Just the constant sound of sand and pebbles settling.

Paulo looked over Miguel's shoulder at the plans. 'Can we get any further round?'

'No. The other walls are solid concrete. We can't smash through them with what we've got.'

Paulo strode forward with his pickaxe. 'Then we dig.'

Miguel set to with his crowbar. Felipe used the other pickaxe. The others took what they could find: Li seized an ancient axe; Amber found a long stick leaning up against the stele. It was covered with carvings but it was good when used like a cricket bat to whack lumps of concrete onto the floor. Alex pulled pieces of masonry away with his good hand.

Paulo dug the axe in and was suddenly thrown violently aside.

He rolled over and looked up. In the incomplete

light from the torches, he saw something he didn't want to see.

Debris was trembling down the heap like it was alive.

Paulo picked himself up. 'Get out,' he yelled. 'It's coming down!'

He raced towards the ladder, the others hard on his heels. Lumps of masonry tumbled after them as they climbed to the hole. In moments they were outside on the grass.

'What happened?' said Amber.

'I don't know,' said Paulo. 'I must have hit something unstable.' Behind him, Miguel and Felipe gasped, getting their breath back.

Li looked through the window using the goggles. The debris was still falling, spreading the pile across the floor like a cold lava flow. It now blocked the hole they'd cut in the wall. 'This is weird,' she said.

She handed Alex the goggles. 'Here, you have a look.'

Alex saw Paulo's pickaxe sticking up. Under it, something was moving, jerking like a big animal trying to surface. What was it? Then he had an idea.

'Felipe, how is that animatronic dinosaur powered? Is it mains or battery?'

'Battery. Why?'

'I think it's come to life. Paulo, look at where your axe is.'

Paulo took the goggles. There was his axe, the handle at forty-five degrees, like a fence post trying to remain upright after a rock fall. And there was an object about three metres long like the tail of a swimming shark. It jerked fitfully and whacked against a square concrete pillar, sending lumps of masonry tumbling. Further up the pile, the jagged pieces of broken wall and ceiling were rocking dangerously.

'My axe must have completed a circuit. It's turned the dinosaur on.'

Miguel was shining his torch in. 'It's destabilizing the entire thing. See that pillar it's hitting? That's holding up what's left of the upper floor.'

Paulo knew what that meant. He gave Li the goggles and turned to climb back in. 'I've got to stop it or it'll bring down everything.'

'Do you think you should go back in?' said Felipe.

But Paulo was already shinning down the ladder. Li, Amber and Alex watched him nervously.

He reached the ground. The end of the tail was five metres away. The pickaxe had gone in high up, around where it met the hind legs. He crept closer and his torch picked out the row of plates along where the top of the spine would be. Some child part of his brain thrilled – it was a stegosaurus! Then something hit him hard and slammed him into the pillar.

Paulo stayed there for a moment, winded. It was like being knocked down by a car.

Li's voice called out. 'Are you OK, Paulo?'

Paulo gasped a couple of times and finally got his lungs working. 'It's really heavy.'

He heard Felipe. 'Of course it is. It's a model of a very big animal.'

Li's voice rang out. 'Watch out!'

Paulo looked behind him. A vicious spiked thing was hurtling towards him. He dived out of the way. It whistled past him, dug into the pillar, then flicked away, leaving a sprinkling of concrete dust. Of course. The stegosaurus had four vicious spikes on its tail. It lashed upwards and Paulo saw ragged masonry tumbling towards him like huge boulders. He pressed himself flat against the pillar, eyes closed. The tail thundered past, missing him by centimetres. If he didn't get that axe out and break the circuit, he'd be buried.

He heard one of the others shout from the window. But it was too late – he screwed up his courage.

He lined up the torch on the axe handle and ran for it. The tail came searing towards him again. His boots scrabbled on the loose rubble and he leaped forwards. As he landed, one of the sharp fibreglass plates along the stegosaurus's spine dug into his chest. But he had to get the job done. He pulled the pickaxe handle.

Just as suddenly as it had started, the monster was still.

Paulo took a breath, seeing if his lungs would inflate. Not too bad. No blood. Amazingly, nothing seemed to be broken.

Li was picking her way towards him, wearing the night vision goggles.

Paulo's face was grinning with delight. 'Hey, frog-woman,' he said, 'I fought a stegosaurus.'

But Li had seen something else. A small glowing glove, rising like Excalibur from the greyish rubble. 'Hey,' she called, 'we've got a survivor!'

Felipe stuck his head through the window. 'Jorges?' he called out.

A shrill voice replied, 'Daddy!'

In moments the group were back down the ladder. Li was already digging, pulling away masonry from where she had seen Jorges's arm. As the others reached her she looked in the hole and saw a face, a miniature Felipe, glowing about half a metre down. His eyes and mouth were wide, white-hot pools of wonder.

'He's all right,' she gasped. 'He's all right. Let's dig.'

Six pairs of hands began to pull debris away. In no time, they had widened the hole. Li reached in and hauled the little boy out.

Felipe hugged him hard, like he would never let go of him again.

The others shone torches into the hole. It was deep; reaching beyond the floor and into the foundations of the basement. Shattered fibreglass and wires mingled with the masonry; the remains of the stegosaurus.

'Paulo,' said Miguel, 'if you hadn't stuck the

pickaxe in the dinosaur tail I don't think we'd have been able to move all this.'

Felipe lowered Jorges. 'Come on, Jorges. Your sister's waiting.'

But as Felipe tried to lead him away he dug his feet in, refusing to move. 'There's somebody in there.'

Li, Paulo, Alex and Amber responded as one: 'In where?'

Jorges pointed back to the wall of rubble. 'In there. He was talking.'

Amber clambered over the masonry. The ceiling debris had fallen away to reveal broken pieces of dinosaur bone, snapped remains of steel cable. 'This is the T. rex!' she shouted. 'The last bit we couldn't get to.'

Paulo and Li began to climb after her. 'Careful, Amber,' called Li. 'That doesn't look very stable.'

'Amber!' shrilled Jorges. 'He said your name.'

'When?'

Jorges shrugged. 'A while ago.'

Amber yelled at the jagged mass of bones. 'Hex! Hex! Are you in there?' She turned round. 'Who's got the goggles?'

'Me. I'm looking now.' Alex was wearing them, scanning the wreckage. Was there the slightest trace of body heat?

Three glowing faces looked at him, the question in their eyes. Are we too late?

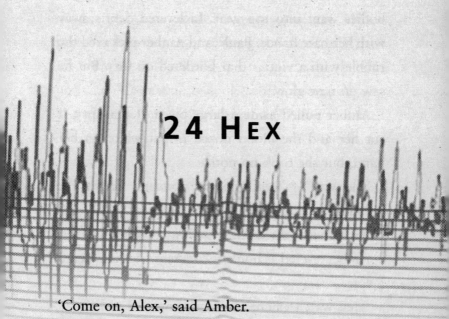

24 HEX

'Come on, Alex,' said Amber.

Alex stared hard. There was no obvious glowing figure like there had been with Jorges, but was that just the faintest wisp of luminance from a person breathing?

It was the only possible clue. He pointed. 'Start digging there.'

Alex kept the goggles on as they pulled the pieces of concrete aside. His three friends were exhausted but they worked like maniacs. Alex watched their glowing figures become brighter and hotter as their bodies went into top gear. Li levered debris away with her bare hands. Paulo and Amber pickaxed the rubble with a vigour that bordered on fury. But he saw no new glow.

Amber pulled aside a large piece of masonry. It cut her and the blood oozed bright white on her hand, but she took no notice.

The wisp of breath became suddenly bright like a flame.

'He's there!' cried Alex, pointing.

Amber levered a chunk of concrete aside and heard a voice.

'Hey, watch where you're putting that pickaxe.'

She flung the axe down and pulled the masonry away with her hands. As it came away it released a strong smell of stale air and sweat.

Hex's face and hair were caked in dust, as though he had been made up to look like a statue. 'Hi,' he grinned. But his eyes behind the smile were hollow and exhausted.

Li peered forwards. The smell hit her nostrils. 'Phew, smells like a Turkish wrestler's armpit in here.'

'Well,' said Hex weakly, 'I have been trying to exercise to keep up my morale.'

Paulo's face was the next that Hex saw. The curly hair and easy smile were the same as ever. 'Hey, *amigo*, what took you so long?'

Shakily Hex got to his feet. It felt weird to stand up; as if he had been permanently moulded into one position, like a doll. It felt unreal. In a minute he'd wake up and he'd be in that airless dark hole again.

Behind Paulo was Alex, still wearing the sling, holding the night vision goggles in his good hand. 'Hey, man, how are you doing?'

'I hope you've been taking care of our toy,' said Hex. He was working on autopilot, talking to people but not really feeling like he was there.

'Is anyone else in there?' Li was peering into the hole. 'Oh,' she said. 'Paulo?' she called.

Hex watched as Paulo climbed past him and into the hole. He found himself talking again. 'She died. There was nothing I could do.' Even that seemed unreal. Surely he'd wake up in a minute.

Paulo pushed some masonry away to make the hole bigger. 'We'd better get her out.'

Li squirmed into the hole. 'No, Paulo,' Hex heard her say in a low voice. 'Jorges might see.' After so long hearing nothing, even the slightest whisper sounded loud. And everyone was so efficient, doing everything so briskly. Hex felt like he was moving in slow motion.

'She's stiff anyway,' said Paulo. 'Been dead for a few hours.' He looked at Hex. 'Are you OK?'

Hex nodded. That felt like autopilot too.

Amber was looking into the hole. 'That's quite a small space you were in.' She looked at the body. 'Who was she?'

'A researcher.' Hex didn't want to talk about it. Amber had a cut on her forehead. Hex kept wanting to look at that instead of her eyes.

Amber nudged him. 'I see you kept yourself busy.'

Hex realized his palmtop was still glowing in his hand. There was a text file open on it; the letter he had been writing. Swiftly, he pressed a key and deleted it.

Amber peered over his shoulder. 'What's that?'

'I'm just saving my game,' said Hex. He closed the palmtop and tucked it away in his belt pack.

In the growing light he could see into the hole. He looked at the body he'd spent so long with. The lolling head. The short dark hair. At least he'd closed her eyes.

'We'll come back for her later,' said Paulo. 'Let's get the others out first.'

Hex followed them to a ladder by a window. There was a big man he didn't recognize and Felipe, the curator, with a mini-Felipe caked with dust like he was. They must have just rescued him.

'Hi, Hex,' said Felipe. 'Good to see you out and about.'

'I've had a good rest while all my mates have been running around,' smiled Hex. It was easier to make jokes with strangers.

Felipe sent Jorges up the ladder first, then went up behind him. The sky was getting lighter.

Miguel watched Felipe exit safely and signalled to Amber and Li to go up ahead of him. 'Ladies first.'

'No,' said Amber. 'You first. You're nearer.'

He was about to object, and not just out of chivalry: it was ingrained as part of his training – get the civilians out first. But he had to hand it to these kids, they seemed as professional as the slickest firefighting team he had worked with. Even the guy who'd been buried all that time – he looked a bit punch drunk, but he was in control and staying with the others, looking for what needed to be done next. Miguel gave Amber a small salute, and gladly climbed the ladder ahead of her.

He disappeared through the window at the top and Alpha Force were alone. Alone – and complete. For a moment, they all looked at each other, seeing four faces – the four people they were closest to in the entire world. No gaps, no one missing. The fatigue of the night was catching up with them. No one could move. No one felt like moving. Outside they heard the first sounds of the dawn chorus.

It was Amber who broke the silence. 'Er – are we going to leave or have a group hug?'

A sound behind them in the gloom shocked them out of immobility. 'Hold it right there.'

The five friends turned. Two figures were approaching them. One of them held a big torch, which threw the area around them into darkness.

They torch came closer, like a searchlight.

'Were you in the quake?' said Alex. 'We've been looking for survivors.'

The men laughed. Paulo caught a glimpse of something metal and shiny reflecting off their torch. A gun.

It was the looters. And they were armed.

Alpha Force knew when to play it safe. They'd been heroic enough for one day. Human life was more important than a few treasures, however old. Slowly, they put up their hands.

The men came closer. 'Stand aside.'

Paulo shrugged. 'Sure.' He stepped away from the ladder.

The others followed.

'Put down your weapons.'

Weapons? Paulo was still carrying a pickaxe. He put it down. Li lowered the night vision goggles to the ground.

The light from the window was growing, lighting the plaster and dust that rose like mist inside the room. The two men approached. One was well built, with broad shoulders and an aggressive attitude like a boxer. He had something in his hand; something wrapped in a sack. The other man was thinner and wiry and held the gun nervously.

When the light allowed them to get a proper look, Alpha Force silently committed details of their appearance to memory. It was habit, as natural as breathing. You never knew if it might be useful.

The boxer shone the light on Alex's sling. He moved it to Amber's face, then Li's. 'It's them,' he said. 'A black girl, a Chinese, an injured guy. They found the tomb robber in the jungle and took him to the police.'

Alex tried to put all his weariness into his voice. 'You just go. We don't care who you are or what you're doing. We've had a long night. We just want to get out and have a long bath.' And he meant it.

'Do them,' said the boxer.

Alex, Paulo, Li, Hex and Amber caught something in his voice. They knew when someone was bluffing – and he wasn't. In all this chaos it would be easy to get away with killing them. Even though it would be obvious that they weren't casualties of the quake, the looters would have no trouble escaping.

The boxer tried to wrap the piece of sacking closer

around the item in his hand. Instead, it fell away. A few rays of the morning sunlight caught what was underneath.

A gleaming piece of gold.

'Oh, look at that mask,' said Amber in a steely voice.

Alex thought, I'm not going to die so that you can take that away.

The thin man put his foot on the bottom rung of the ladder to block their escape. There was a click. He'd cocked the gun.

Hex kicked away the ladder viciously. The thin man lost his balance and the gun went off, the bullet pinging off the ceiling.

Li and Paulo charged at the boxer and knocked him to the ground. Amber went for the mask.

Alex thought about an escape route. They couldn't use the window and they couldn't go back through the hole in the wall because it was blocked. He still had the fireman's plans but there wasn't time to get them out. He tried to remember them. There was another way out, he thought, past this main work-shop area. Probably where the looters had come from.

The thin man was groaning and rolling on the ground. Li and Paulo had disabled him. Now was their chance.

Alex grabbed the night vision goggles and pulled them on. He saw the thin man lunging for his gun. His eyes and open mouth glowed demonically white as his fingers closed on the weapon.

Alex snapped a spine off the tail of the fibreglass stegosaurus. With a flick of the wrist he frisbeed it towards the thin man. It sliced into his hand like a knife. The gun clattered to the ground and spun away into the shadows.

Paulo and Li had dropped the torches. One rolled towards Alex and he grabbed it. He flashed it twice then turned it off. The others knew what that meant. Come with me, now.

They got up and ran.

Alex kept the torch turned off. It would give away their position and anyway he was wearing the goggles. He led the way through the green, rubble-strewn room and into a corridor. It was the warren of rooms where ancient treasures were stored. The others pounded behind.

Alex consulted the map in his head. Not that turning. The next. And then out the other side and round in a circle to double back and confuse their pursuers.

They were lucky. The rooms were still intact. Maybe they'd all survived because they were small and weren't trying to support a large ceiling over a big empty space. Alex was wiry and fast, darting like a fish through room after room. The others stayed on his heels, trusting him and keeping close.

The looters behind fired a shot. Alex turned the group and the bullet ricocheted in an empty room. His tactic was working. The looters didn't know where he was going, couldn't see them because they weren't using a torch.

Alex, able to see clearly, was leading them on a magical mystery tour. He passed a giant head the size of a demolition ball. Huge bulbous eyes stared at him. The next room held the skeletons of tiny dinosaurs in a glass case, arranged like flying fairies. A stele lay in pieces in the next one, as if it had been sawn up for a stage magic act.

Suddenly he was plunged into darkness. He groped

out blindly and crashed into a wall. Amber cannoned into him. Li, Paulo and Hex breathed heavily behind him.

They huddled into a group. They had to talk. They tried to do it in the faintest of whispers.

Alex ripped the goggles off his head.

'Battery gone?' hissed Hex.

'Must be,' panted Alex.

Another volley of shots rang out.

'How far?' whispered Amber.

Alex tried to remember the map in his head. 'Not far. This way,' he whispered. 'But the moment we put the torches on they'll see us so we'll have to run like hell.'

Alex put the torch on.

It was like a starter pistol. They started running, as fast as they could.

Behind them, the robbers saw the beams and began to fire intensively. A volley of shots rang out close to Alex's ear. That was uncomfortably close.

Ahead was a long room with a heavy wooden door. Alex dived in.

Hex, the last through, pushed it shut.

'Block the entrance,' yelled Alex.

Paulo, Li and Amber pushed a heavy wooden chest against it.

Alex pointed his torch into the room. It was long and wide, like an airport corridor. But a dark wooden door stood at the end. 'Over there,' called Alex.

They ran towards it. The door was huge, like the entrance to a palace. Grand carvings in the distinctive Maya style covered every surface.

'Oh, that's rather fine,' said Amber. 'I don't suppose it leads to the lavatory.' She was still clutching the mask in its sacking cover.

Another shot rang out. The looters were at the door at the other end of the room.

'Alex, while you're admiring the carving,' said Paulo, 'I think we'd better get out.'

'I'm actually trying to find the handle,' said Alex. 'Ah, there.' He turned it and pushed.

Nothing happened. It wouldn't move.

As one, the five friends put their shoulders to the door and pushed.

It was no good.

Paulo dropped to his knees and looked through

the gap between the two great slabs of wood. 'I can see daylight. 'We can definitely get out.' He shoved it with his shoulder. 'Only it won't budge.'

'Is it locked?'

'I can't see a lock. We just can't move it.'

Another shot.

Alex threw the map down and handed the torch to Amber. With his good hand he opened his belt kit. He got something out and handed it to Hex.

Hex knew by the feel of it what it was – a stick of plastic explosive. 'Are you sure?'

There was a rat-a-tat of bullets as the looters shot into the door.

'Has anyone got any better ideas?'

'Have you got the other bits too?' asked Li.

Alex opened another pocket on his belt pack. In it he had the white coil of det cord, the box of detonators and some wire. He went up to the door and looked at it.

A sickening crunch of wood made them all look back towards the other door. The looters must be trying to batter their way in.

'Hex, can you break that stick into three.'

Hex stripped off the cellophane and snapped the stick neatly into three pieces.

Alex took a piece and moulded it into a blob, like putty. 'We need a piece on each hinge. Make sure the surface is clean or it won't stick.' Alex put his piece into the lock.

Hex and Amber cleaned the dust off the hinges and set the other two charges, pushing them in well.

One-handed, Alex hooked the box of detonators out of his pack. Li was ready to assist. 'One in each?' she said.

Yeah.' Alex nodded. 'Be careful. The heat from your—'

'– hands can set them off,' finished Li. 'I remember. And trees might be bigger than you thought.'

That was just what Alex needed right now. His smashed fingers were all too fresh a reminder of the mistakes he made last time. He had to forget that now, and just remember his training. But this time it was all the more crucial. If he got it wrong, the pressure wave would kill them as surely as a falling roof . . .

Crash. The looters were really laying into the door. This was no time to have doubts. Alex gave the det cord to Paulo. 'Take my knife. Connect the detonators like this.' With his toe he drew a diagram in the dust on the floor.

Li had put the detonators in the blobs of explosive. Paulo added the det cord.

'How do we set it off?' asked Hex.

'The firing device. It's in my belt pack.' Alex held up his hands so that Hex could see into the pouches.

'There's just these in there,' said Hex. He brought out a couple of twisted wires like stripped electrical cable.

Alex swore. 'Where's the firing device? It must be somewhere.' He started looking around on the floor.

At the far end of the room, the door was starting to bow. Soon it would give.

'What exactly does it do?' said Paulo.

'Provides a charge that sets everything off.'

Amber said, 'We can't look for it now. Hex, your palmtop.'

'We can't use that. There's no signal.'

Amber groaned and Alex suddenly realized what she was driving at. 'No, but we can use the battery. Quick.'

Hex got out the device and levered off the battery lid. 'That's an expensive piece of equipment—'

Amber plucked the battery out of the black machine. 'Yeah, then it should do the job.'

Alex took a deep breath and twisted the wires onto the det cord. The door at the far end gave a splintering crunch. The looters were nearly through the barricade.

Alex straightened up. Had he done everything? Was it all going to work? Had he judged the weight of the door correctly?

Only one way to find out.

'What happens if you get it wrong?' said Amber.

Alex grinned. 'Another earthquake.'

'Really?'

'No, it'll just kill us all. That's how my dad's best friend was killed.'

'Right, everyone stand along the wall next to the door.'

They lined up beside him.

'Put your hands over your ears and open your mouth. Otherwise the pressure wave will burst your teeth.' He put the palmtop battery on the floor in front of him, then straightened up. 'Ready?'

Li, Amber, Hex and Paulo put their hands over their ears and flattened themselves against the wall.

Now or never. Alex touched the wires to the battery, then ducked and wrapped his good arm around his head.

They saw the flash before they heard the noise. The noise was huge, but at the same time strangely silent. It was like being inside a giant bell and being vaguely aware that it had been rung, but too deafened to hear it. Plaster was falling all around them, and then that all too familiar sound. Ripping, crumbling concrete.

The double doors were wide open. That was all they needed to see.

They ran. Plaster showered down from the ceiling. Concrete fell from the weakened structure. It was like the beginning of the evening; dinosaur bones falling everywhere. Hex had a peculiar feeling of déjà vu. Had he ever actually got out of the pit with the dead girl? What are you running for? his brain asked. You'll never get away. He slowed as the debris came down around him like rain.

Amber saw Hex just standing still. She cannoned into him, shouldering him on like a buffalo in mid charge. 'Move your ass, Hex,' she shrieked. 'Get out.'

Hex realized he really had got out of the pit. The girl had died, but he had survived. And he was in danger right now.

He ran like he had never run in his life. Towards the morning sky. Behind him, the roof collapsed and buried the looters in a great roar.

25 MORNING

The sun was up. Parents were arriving all the time, driving battered vehicles laden with emergency supplies. They hugged their children, then packed them into the car and headed out of the ruined city. Señora Marquez presided over her dwindling class aided by her temporary assistants – Jose, Imelda, Miguel, Thalia and Felipe and Alpha Force.

Inside Miguel's van, Amber swiftly injected her insulin, packed her kit away and came out to join the others. Alex moved the night vision goggles onto his lap to make room for her to sit down and Paulo handed her a coffee.

Li looked up into the sky. 'You know – it sounds like things are getting back to normal.' The air was no longer full of the wail of sirens. Instead it was peaceful with just the occasional car or truck going past.

Two fire trucks stood on the grass, next to the ragged hole the girder had made in the front wall of the museum. Firemen were inside, looking for the trapped looters. The building was a ruin; the roof collapsed, the other walls cracked.

Alex nudged Amber. 'Some other things are getting back to normal too.'

Amber smiled. Hex had his palmtop open and was fingering the keys. She leaned over. 'I thought your battery had gone.'

'I had a spare,' said Hex, not looking up. 'Mind that cable, by the way.'

Amber looked down. A black wire snaked out of Hex's palmtop and through to the front of the van. He was charging the machine from the cigarette lighter socket on the dashboard. Amber tried to peer at the screen. 'So, what's going on?'

Hex raised his finger and did a quiet countdown. 'Three – two – one – now.'

The moment he said, 'Now,' an electronic chorus chirped up. Ringing, warbling, beeping – the phones were suddenly live again. Hex grinned at his four friends as the group in front of them all did the same thing – gasped and searched their pockets for their handsets. In moments they were chatting or texting, their faces shining with relief. The world was creeping back to normal.

'I was watching the service providers' website,' said Hex.

'Anything else going on?' said Paulo.

'Yeah, I've got Reuters, the news agency.' Hex read off the screen. '*Belize City is reeling after a massive earthquake last night. The quake struck at ten p.m. local time and measured eight point five on the Richter scale. Emergency services were overwhelmed as tremors caused widespread damage to buildings and roads. Experts say it's too early to estimate the extent of the catastrophe but the loss of life is expected to be in the thousands.'*

Another car pulled up, its back end low on its axles. Through the glass of the hatchback Alpha Force could see blankets, bottles of water and tinned food. Alejandro, the boy Paulo had saved with the kiss of life, went to hug his parents as they climbed out of the car. Another family reunited.

Li peered over Hex's shoulder. She noticed a head-line further down the page. 'AMAZING FIND IN ANCIENT TOMB MAY BE A THOUSAND YEARS OLD, SAY EXPERTS.' It seemed like another thousand years since they'd found it.

Felipe snapped his phone shut and strode towards them. His overcoat swung as he walked, revealing the gold mask tucked into his inside pocket. He hadn't let it out of his sight since Amber had given it back to him. 'Hey, guys,' he said. 'I've just been talking to the museum board. I'm trying to get together an expedition to the tomb in the jungle.' He shrugged. 'After all, we're going to need a few new decorations round here. Would you be interested in coming along?'

Five faces looked at him eagerly. 'Yes!' 'Absolutely!' 'You bet!' 'Right now?'

'Ow,' squealed Amber, and doubled over.

Hex looked at her with concern. 'What's wrong?'

Amber's voice was muffled as she rolled up her trouser leg. 'Just this bite. It's quite big and swollen.'

'Let me see,' said Felipe. 'I've had a few bites in my time.'

Amber presented Felipe with the evidence. 'I'm a diabetic,' she explained. 'I don't heal well.'

Jorges and Ana came up to have a look too. 'Eww,' said Ana. 'Bots.'

Felipe looked at his daughter. 'It certainly is.'

'Bots?' repeated Paulo. 'Like horses get?' His face was disgusted.

'Oh my,' said Li. 'Nasty.' She looked more closely. 'Ooh, it really is.'

'Oh brother,' groaned Amber.

Felipe, Ana, Jorges and Li were bending over Amber's leg like detectives over a clue.

'Is that the tail?' said Li. 'That white thing moving in there?'

'Yes,' said Jorges.

'Moving?' repeated Amber. 'Tail? You mean there's something alive in there?'

'Yes, you've got a larva in there,' said Felipe. 'See that little white circle? That's its breathing hole.'

'Oh how gross!' groaned Amber. 'Can you pull it out?'

'No,' said Paulo. 'It will burst. After a few weeks it will hatch. Then it should heal with no problem.'

Alex and Hex exchanged horrified looks. 'A few weeks,' said Alex.

'It's like *Alien*,' said Hex.

Amber fixed her tormentors with a fierce stare. 'I am not waiting while it hatches! There must be something you can do.'

'You can suffocate them with Vaseline,' said Felipe. 'Indians sometimes put a piece of raw meat on them to tempt them out.'

'Ow!' Amber jumped again.

'That's it feeding on the tissues in your leg,' said Ana calmly.

'Really?' said Hex. He tried to peer over Li's shoulder. 'Let me see.'

'If no one's got a steak,' said Amber through gritted teeth, 'shall we give it some bagel? Or shall we all just stand here and look at it?' She felt another

stab of pain, and fingers prodding the bite. 'Ow –
Jorges, don't poke it, you'll make it angry.'

Jorges put his thumbs either side of the bite and
pushed. A thing shot out of the hole, missing Li's
ear by centimetres. A white maggot landed on the
grass and squirmed in the daylight.

'All gone,' said Jorges.

Felipe looked at his son, amazed. 'Where did you
learn to do that?'

'From the Indians in Lubaantun,' said Jorges.

'Felipe,' said Amber, 'we'll come to the jungle
with you on one condition – you bring Jorges.'

'Done!' said Felipe.

The white maggot curled up in the sun. It was just
one of the many souvenirs the five friends carried of
the past few days. Cuts, bruises; grey dust daubed
their torn jungle clothing like woad. Paulo had fine
pieces of plaster in his curly mop. Amber had a mess
of dried blood across her forehead and a fresh, bleeding
wound on her leg. Li had a vertical line of plaster and
rust down the middle of her body where she'd ridden
the girder out through the wall. Hex had his grey statue
make-up, his clothes stiff and white like plaster of

Paris, Susana's blood drying on his face like freckles. Alex had his bandage and sling. In just over twelve hours it had become as ragged and grubby as the makeshift bandage Paulo had put on him in the jungle.

'Hey, guys,' said Alex, 'if we go back to the tomb we can pick up our navigation exercise where we left off—'

'Can't,' said Hex swiftly. He nodded at the ruined museum. 'Our equipment's gone.'

'I bet not all of it has,' said Paulo darkly. 'Alex's bergen will be all right.'

'Yeah,' said Li bitterly.

'The whole place could fall down but that bergen will be all right,' said Amber.

'I got that bergen for my birthday,' said Alex mildly.

'Your birthday?' repeated Li. She looked mischievously at the others. They caught her cue.

Four pairs of eyes glared at Alex. He remembered very well the last time they all looked at him like that. It was when they were throwing water on the signal fire in the jungle.

'I think,' said Li, 'we'd better give Alex the bumps.'

CHRIS RYAN'S TOP SAS TIPS ON SURVIVING EARTHQUAKES

Some parts of the world are prone to earthquakes. They're not always on a disastrous scale, but even minor tremors can cause injuries if you're in the wrong place at the wrong time – plus they're very frightening! However, if you know what to do you can protect yourself, your family and your mates from injury.

Here are my top tips for surviving an earthquake.

1. DON'T MISS WARNING SIGNS
If you are in an area of the world where earthquakes are common, the authorities will usually

have equipment set up to register when a quake is coming so that they can then warn the population. So if you're staying in an earthquake zone, do find out how warnings are normally announced in that area. This could be on TV or radio, but there may also be websites you can keep an eye on.

When I was on an undercover mission in Tokyo, where experts are permanently on alert for a major quake, everyone knew that if they heard all the police sirens in the city sound in 45-second bursts it was time to take cover. I always kept a pair of shoes by the bed just in case.

2. KNOW THE LOCAL PLANS

Again, if you're in a city or other built-up area, the disaster authorities will have made plans. In Tokyo, they were mega-organized – all the locals knew which parts of the transport system would still be working, which areas of the city would be evacuated and cordoned off, and which roads would be closed. Make sure you know too. You don't want to find yourself running around like a headless chicken when everyone else is calmly walking to the subway station!

3. MAKE YOUR ENVIRONMENT SAFE

You may be injured by falling and flying objects. Hotels and other public places should have been designed and furnished with this in mind, and will have their own procedures, so read the safety drills and follow them. However, if you're staying in someone's house you can help them by spotting potential hazards.

- Secure tall and heavy furniture such as cabinets and bookcases to walls.
- Shut away small appliances, like toasters and kettles – or you could do what some people in Tokyo did and secure them to a shelf or worktop with Velcro.
- If possible, take down heavy-framed pictures and mirrors in case they fall on you.
- Put large and heavy objects on lower shelves and put breakable items such as bottles or glass and china in cabinets with latches – but ask permission before nailing your auntie's furniture to the wall and hiding her ornaments in a cupboard!
- Make sure everyone knows how and when to

call the police, ambulance or fire brigade and which radio station to tune into for emergency information.

- Everyone in the group also needs to know where and how to shut off electricity, gas and water in case they are damaged during the quake. The local telephone book may carry instructions on where to find main switches and valves. Do you know where your water stopcock at home is? If not, ask your parent or guardian to show you, for this is something you could practise – stopcocks can be stiff and you need to know how hard to turn and when the supply really is off. Warn everyone before trying, though – you wouldn't appreciate it if you were under the shower with a headful of shampoo and the water suddenly stopped!

4. PUT TOGETHER AN EMERGENCY SURVIVAL KIT

Water supplies and electricity may be knocked out by the quake, so make sure you can cope.

Collect and store the following:

- 3 gallons of bottled water per person

- Non-perishable food such as dried items and cans – and don't forget a non-electric can opener!
- Make sure you've got at least one powerful torch with spare batteries.
- A portable radio (again, one that runs off batteries, with spares)
- Tools (particularly an adjustable spanner for turning off utilities)
- Blankets
- Sturdy shoes
- Sanitary items, like a loo roll, toothpaste and some soap
- A first aid kit is essential too – and brush up on your first aid and CPR skills. Every member of Alpha Force knows at least basic first aid and the essential life-saving skills and it is well worth learning these for yourself. Why not ask at your school or local library and find out if there are any courses in your area? It could mean the difference between life and death for someone at some point. Injuries in earthquake situations may include crush injuries (like the trapped teacher), fractures, cuts and bruises from flying glass and

other debris and, of course, shock, which can kill.

- If anyone in your group, such as babies or disabled people, needs special items, make sure these are to hand – not left in the bathroom where you might not be able to reach them. The same goes for prescription medicines – like the insulin Amber needs for her diabetes.

- A portable fire escape ladder might come in very handy – check it's working, though.

- Lastly, don't forget cash, warm and protective clothing, rainwear and sleeping bags.

5. TAKING COVER WHEN THE QUAKE STARTS

If you're outside, stay outside. If you're indoors, stay there. During earthquakes, most people are injured when they try to get into or out of buildings.

If you're outside, move away from trees, signs, buildings, bridges, underpasses and utility wires. Ideally you shouldn't shelter in a doorway or by a wall as debris might fall on you, but if you're in a street and can't get to an open space it may be better than nothing. Once you've chosen your spot, stay there until the shaking stops. Unless you're in immediate danger, don't change your mind and run to a new doorway to see if it's safer – you could get hurt on the way! Wrap your arms around your head, protecting your skull and eyes.

If you're inside, remember the following rule:

Duck, Cover and Hold.

- DUCK under a sturdy desk or table. Remember how Li protects herself by diving under a table in the canteen area of the museum, and Ana and her friends hide in an opened safe down in the basement.
- If no desk or table is available, seek COVER against an inside wall (not an outside wall – and not an interior wall with glass) and protect your head and neck with your arms.
- HOLD onto the desk or table. If it moves, move with it. Hold the position until the ground stops shaking and it is safe to move.

Stay away from windows, bookcases, filing cabinets, tall furniture, heavy mirrors, hanging plants, and anything that could fall. Watch out for falling plaster or ceiling tiles. Also stay away from internal doorways. Although people used to be advised to shelter there, you could get your fingers crushed in the door if you're not positioned properly.

If you're in the kitchen, move away from the fridge, stove, and overhead cupboards.

If you're in a crowded shop or other public place, don't run for exits as stairways may be broken or jammed with people. Never use lifts as the power may fail. Move away from shelves or dangerous items on walls.

Find something solid to take cover under; if you're in a stadium or cinema duck between the seats and cover your head. Wait until the shaking stops before trying to leave.

Don't be surprised if the fire alarm or sprinklers come on. If there is an evacuation plan, follow the instructions of the person in charge.

If you're in a wheelchair, stay in it and move to

cover. If possible, lock your wheels, and protect your head with your arms.

If you're in a car, you might get bounced around a lot on its shock absorbers. Although this is very scary, it's actually safe – so long as the driver has pulled over to the side of the road, and stopped well away from bridges, underpasses and utility poles. Don't forget to turn the radio on for emergency information. You did keep a note of the station in the car as well as in the house, didn't you?

6. PRACTISE EMERGENCY DRILLS

If you know a quake may be coming, practise going for shelter – and encourage the others in your group to do so as well. Identify safe spots and look for the danger spots too. If you've planned where you're going to go and what to do, you'll find it a lot easier when everything's shaking and you're scared stiff!

Think about what you would do if a quake happens when your group isn't all together. If you know one is coming, you could set up an emergency contact number, such as a relative or friend well away from the earthquake zone. Then you all phone in from wherever you are and report that you're safe. Check that the person you call is aware they've been nominated, though – while your mum would appreciate being told you're OK, she may not realize she's also a switchboard operator for all your mates!

7. AFTERWARDS

- Stay calm. This is really important as panic can cause further injuries, as well as upsetting other survivors. When Alex finds himself trapped under the dinosaur skeleton, he uses his head and thinks about his situation before deciding in which direction to dig to give himself the best chance of getting free. If he had just panicked and dug madly in any direction, he could have used up valuable energy to no effort.

- Check yourself for injuries and protect yourself from further harm by putting on long trousers, a long-sleeved shirt, sturdy shoes and work gloves, if they are available.

- Check others for injuries and give them first aid, if necessary. Get everyone together, but do not try to move anyone who's seriously injured unless they are in immediate danger. Remember that babies, the elderly and people with disabilities may need special help.

- Make sure there is no smell of gas. If there is, open windows and shut off the main gas valve – and don't light any matches or candles or turn on any lights! Also check electricity supplies and water lines – you may have to shut these off too.

- Turn on your battery-powered radio and listen for important information such as road closures, damage and evacuation centres.

- Check telephone receivers are back on their cradles – they may have been knocked off and if you leave them like that it may disrupt the service.

- If water pipes are damaged, shut off the supply at the main valve. Extra emergency drinking water may be obtained from water heaters or melted ice cubes. Check to see that sewage lines are intact before using the loo!

- If you are trapped, do anything you possibly can to attract attention. Call for help or wave something eye-catching – that horrible yellow swirly scarf your gran gave you last Christmas might come in very handy! If you have a mobile and it is working, use that. Otherwise, though, stay off the phone unless you have to report an emergency.

- Remember that the emergency services will be working to find you if you are trapped under rubble or in a collapsed building. If you are in a group, remind others of this too. It's amazing how quickly morale can lift in a group if at least one person is confident of rescue.

8. OUTSIDE

If you were outside when the quake struck, whether in a car or on foot, stay away from bridges – they might be damaged. Be careful when going near buildings, and try not to go into any that are damaged.

9. HELPING OTHERS

If you've got out safely, you might be able to lend a hand to others. In really serious quakes many of the rescuers have been members of the public who've joined in with the digging. But try and stay close to other people, and don't be a hero – never put yourself in danger.

And remember – saving lives is important, but never go back into an unstable building simply to collect any lost belongings, or valuables. After the earthquake in the museum, Alpha Force are immediately focused on survivors and rescuing victims – not finding the golden mask, even though it is extremely valuable.

10. GETTING BACK TO NORMAL

If you're staying in someone's house, they might need your help to get ship-shape again.

Check all bottles such as medicines, bleaches or flammable liquids – they might have spilled. When you open cupboard doors, do so carefully – items will have shifted. You might come through the quake unscathed and then be buried under an avalanche of china or baked bean cans!

Inspect the entire house for gas leaks, damage to the electrical system, and sewerage and water line damage. If damage of this kind goes unnoticed it could cause a fire.

Be prepared for aftershocks! Although most of these are smaller than the main tremor, some may be strong enough to cause extra damage or bring weakened structures down. Aftershocks can occur in the first hours, days, weeks, or even months after the quake.

Also be prepared to comfort others in your group. Earthquakes are very upsetting and although people may look fine initially, especially while they have a mess to sort out, they may suddenly get shaky or upset. Younger children especially may need to talk about their feelings. You can help reassure them.

Big quakes are rare and happily the big one didn't hit Tokyo when I was there. But I felt a lot better for knowing exactly what I'd do if it did.

BE SAFE!

Chris Ryan

Random House Children's Books and Chris Ryan would like to make it clear that these tips are for use in a serious situation only, where your life may be at risk. We cannot accept any liability for inappropriate usage in normal conditions.

About the Author

Chris Ryan joined the SAS in 1984 and has been involved in numerous operations with the Regiment. During the first Gulf War he was the only member of an eight-man team to escape from Iraq, three colleagues being killed and four captured. It was the longest escape and evasion in the history of the SAS. For this he was awarded the Military Medal. He wrote about his remarkable escape in the adult bestseller *The One Who Got Away* (1995), which was also adapted for screen.

He left the SAS in 1994 and is now the author of many bestselling thrillers for adults, as well as the *Alpha Force* series for younger readers. His work in security takes him around the world and he has also appeared in a number of television series, including *Hunting Chris Ryan*, in which his escape and evasion skills were demonstrated to the max, and *Pushed to the Limit*, in which Chris put ordinary British families through a series of challenges. On Sky TV he also appeared in *Terror Alert*, demonstrating his skills in a range of different scenarios.

Don't miss Alpha Force's next mission –
in the Caribbean . . .

ALPHA FORCE

Target: Assassin!

BLACK GOLD

The five members of Alpha Force are training in the
Caribbean when an oil tanker runs aground, spilling
oil – black gold – into the seas.

Diving down to the stricken tanker, Alpha Force soon
discover that all is not as it seems. But they will need
all their skills and ingenuity – powerboating, scuba
diving, jet skiing – when a bomb explodes and an
assassin strikes . . .

ISBN 0 099 48232 0